# MILES'
# SONG

# MILES' SONG

## ALICE McGILL

AN
**APPLE**
PAPERBACK

SCHOLASTIC INC.

New York   Toronto   London   Auckland   Sydney
Mexico City   New Delhi   Hong Kong   Buenos Aires

No part of this publication may be reproduced in whole or in part, or stored in a
retrieval system, or transmitted in any form or by any means, electronic, mechanical,
photocopying, recording, or otherwise, without written permission of the publisher.
For information regarding permission, write to Permissions, Houghton Mifflin
Company, 215 Park Avenue South, New York, NY 10003.

ISBN 0-439-28070-2

Copyright © 2000 by Alice McGill. All rights reserved. Published by Scholastic
Inc., 555 Broadway, New York, NY 10012, by arrangement with Houghton Mifflin
Company. SCHOLASTIC, APPLE PAPERBACKS, and associated logos are
trademarks and/or registered trademarks of Scholastic Inc.

12 11 10 9 8 7 6 5 4 3 2 1          2 3 4 5 6 7/0

Printed in the U.S.A.          40

First Scholastic printing, February 2002

The text of this book is set in 13-point Centaur.

*To my husband and best friend for listening to my story. To my daughters, Paulette and Gwendolyn for understanding my need to write. A special thanks to my editor, Amy. She knew that I could when I wasn't so sure.*

# MILES'
# SONG

# Chapter 1

Miles woke up. Broom straw shavings, swept by an early morning breeze, whirled around his pallet. He looked over from his side of Mama Cee's one-room cabin, rubbing the chill bumps that were popping out on his arms and legs. His Mama Cee had gone to tote water for the washerwomen up at the great house already. She forgot to close the door behind herself. Last night, before he went to bed, she told him she would talk to Ol' Miss about his trouble.

Miles had been banished from the great house the day before for "opening a book," they said. He was scared.

"When she comin' back?" he worried, knowing she would have to rush off to the baby nursery soon after her return.

"Maybe she can't make it right so I can stay up there."

That day was Tuesday, the day he was to find out what was to become of him. Slaves caught looking in books on the Tillery Plantation risked being sold away or maybe even put to death. Slowly, he sat up on his pallet and wrapped a skimpy blanket about his thin shoulders. Mama Cee said he was tall for his age. His twelve-year-old body drooped in the half-darkness.

It was late September 1851. Miles was a slave. Now for the first time in his life he asked why over and over. Up until the day before, field hands and all others who did not work in the great house were slaves, not him. He was a servant-in-training at the great house of Gency Tillery.

"They picked you," his Mama Cee had said happily when he went into training, "'cause you a smart boy and you gonna have nothin' but good bread in your mouth."

Gency Tillery was the richest man in South Carolina. Even the town of Tillery was named after his granddaddy. Hundred-year-old oak trees lined the sandy driveway that led up to his thirty-room mansion with twelve gables. For every gable, there was a decorated fireplace. Miles used to gaze in awe at the lifelike paintings over the mantels. From there, men in great cloaks and women in brocade frocks seemed to stare down into his eyes while he polished the dark wood panels.

He was proud to be a servant-in-training in the great house. "If only I could dust off my mind like the big tables," he now thought, not able to choose between anger and fear. He knew he could not dust his mind like a shiny table. That did not stop him from dreaming about it though. Unconsciously, he rocked back and forth like the old and feeble who looked to whomever had the time to hand them a drink of water.

"What ye doin' dere, boy?" a loud, deep voice flashed into his thoughts like a stroke of lightning. Miles' head jerked up so fast he heard his neck bone crack. There, snaked around the doorjamb, was the shape of Bounty's wizened head.

"Not doin' nothin'," Miles grumbled in the direction of the used-to-be slave tracker. Next to Gency Tillery, funny-talking Bounty was the most feared and whispered about man on the plantation. Bounty was a slave himself, too, though now too old to track runaways anymore. No one knew where he slept at night.

The boy scowled at him from the safety of the cabin, "Said I ain't doin' nothin'," hoping that would send Bounty away.

Bounty's whiskers worked up and down with a stiff warning. "Well, ye best do somethin', 'cause Cee be back heah nigh. If she ketch you sittin' dere studyin' like your mind done unhinged...." The bandy-legged little man turned on his heels, heading toward the great house to refill the kindling boxes for the fireplaces.

Paying no attention to Bounty's gravelly words, Miles plunged back into the depths of his fretful thoughts. He missed his best friends, Jacob and Napoleon, and the great house. They called themselves "Jake, Nape, and Miles." He remembered the day they all started training at the great house when they were five or six years old.

Now it was near time for them to roll out of their soft beds, up in the attic where Miles used to sleep. About ten servants-in-training slept in that part of the house, males and females, aged five to fifteen years old. On the other side of the house, a woman and a man oversaw ten more servants-in-training.

Miles could not stop his past life from running through his memory like a good dream. Even in the rundown cabin with its rickety chimney his senses picked up the sights and smells, tastes and sounds of the great house.

Mrs. Bethenia trained them, a round, kindly-voiced woman with a gray hair or two that was hidden most of the time by her starched head wrap. She had never married, but they always put a handle on her name. Her helper was addressed as Macon, a tall, raw-boned man with coal black eyes.

"Say, 'if you please and thank you,'" Mrs. Bethenia corrected them at the servants' breakfast table, while passing a dish of hot grits or smoked sausage.

Miles relished the taste of the strong, hot coffee that Macon let them sip from his cup to spite Mrs. Bethenia when she turned her back.

"Coffee will make children dull-witted," she would refuse when they begged for a cup of their own.

Miles was trained to walk noiselessly up and down the attic steps and along the servant hallway where Macon showed them how to balance small trays and dishes in the palm of the hand. After that Miles practiced sorting forks, spoons, and knives. He ironed handkerchiefs and napkins and polished the brass doorknobs, and he was ready to answer the bell cord with Macon day or night.

Now, a soft tapping made him look toward the open door again.

"Yo' Mama Cee back yit?" a youngish woman Miles did not recognize asked in a whisper.

"She still up there," he answered, not whispering.

The woman hesitated before she whispered again.

"Well, tell her my baby be bad off sick last night. If she rub 'im down wid gypsum leaves, I thank her."

In a flash the woman was gone. Miles thought again of the other servants at the great house. He could see Mrs. Bethenia fussing with the young girls' apron bows and head wraps. Macon's pressed black cloak would be hanging on his bedpost while he made sure the boys' buckled shoes didn't have mud crusted around the soles.

"You're not slaves, you are servants in Gency Tillery's great house," Mrs. Bethenia and Macon bragged. None of them called the slaveholder "Marse," meaning master, among themselves. They were all in training to be servants for life though.

Miles came back to the present and fretted out loud, "Why they do this to me? I didn't do nothin' but wipe off the books like Macon told me. That book fell by itself."

Just then, a bell tolled to wake a hundred field hands who were cramped, by family, into the few rows of one-room cabins. The second bell would call them to the fields.

"Be glad you don't have to work in the field," Macon used to say when the faint sound of the bell floated up to the attic rooms. Miles had ignored the irritating bell. Now the tone of it lingered in his ears.

He did not have to obey the urgent voices of the shadows that darted past Mama Cee's door. They seemed like scared rabbits as they aroused family and friends from oversleeping. Mothers and older sisters were scrambling to throw together a meal of sweet potatoes, pork skins, and cornmeal. This meager foodstuff was rationed out to them at the end of each week. Sometimes a jug of blackstrap molasses was added.

Slowly, a new mess of feelings saddened him again. He had never been accused of anything before. Mama Cee had always praised him for telling the truth and keeping his hands off of things that did not belong to him. Doubt and fear gnawed at the muscles in his stomach. He had lost what the older field hands called a "good livin' p'sition."

"Dat boy's in high cotton," they had told his Mama Cee, meaning he didn't have to bend his back when he worked.

Miles looked down at his tattered clothes. Macon had snatched away his starched white shirt and fine, light wool knee britches like he was taking from a dog. All of the servants, even Napoleon and Jake, stood at the back window and watched him leave wearing nothing but a pair of rough-sewn pantaloons and a collarless shirt. No more good eats in the house servants' kitchen.

Macon had echoed the plantation's law to all of them many times.

"If a servant offends you one day, sell him or put him in the ground the next day."

Like a fast-growing vine, the news of Miles' trouble had stretched from the library to the upstairs servants. From there, it traveled to the downstairs servants. Then to the cooks who told the gardeners and cobblers and the menfolk at the stables. From there, the news went up and down every cotton row. The vine kept growing until it reached the ditch diggers who paused in knee-deep mud to ponder the news.

That same evening, at dusk, the juicy news spilled out of the field hands' mouths in whispers and sighs outside Mama Cee's cabin. Miles had strained his ears to hear them pass his doom through their lips. He put meanings to the sounds of their words.

"I heered tell he let 'em catch him up there tryin' to make out what was in them books," one said, meaning he should have opened the book but not have gotten caught.

"Dey holding him in the lockup?" one asked tearfully, as if he was her child, meaning if so, he was sure to die or be sold.

"He a fine boy—ain't never had nothin' but a soft bed since he was four, five years old," meaning it was his own fault. "Ol' Marse gonna sell him off."

Suddenly, the thought of losing Mama Cee made Miles jam his eyelids together. "I ain't gonna cry," he said to himself.

Mama Cee was the only mama Miles knew. All of the slave children called her Mama Cee, but he felt like he belonged to her. No mama or papa had come with him when he was brought to the Tillery Plantation as a yearling baby. That meant he had been weaned; that he could take a few steps without falling. Mama Cee took him as her very own.

Even back then she was too old to work at the great house anymore except to tote water and tend the fire around the huge cauldrons for the washerwomen.

The rough sheet that divided his space from that of Mama Cee billowed out at him from an overhanging wire. For about five minutes he gazed through the gaping door at an eerie light threading its way across the edge of the sky.

"I wish I could fly," he blurted out loud. Just as quickly he laughed at the foolish wish.

The second bell tolled just as Mama Cee plodded through the cabin door. Miles could easily make out her tall frame and stooped shoulders. Wispy, white hair curled itself from under her lopsided head wrap. He put a smile on his face and waited for her news.

"I see you's awake," she gushed as she made her way on the other side of the sheet. Miles could hear her kindling a fire in the chimney. Soon she would press her cook pots into the red-hot coals.

"You best get up from there," she called out cheerfully. "You know Jack Frost killed Mister Green Man last night? It gonna be a nice, sunshiny day." She added, "Still good cotton pickin' weather, cool nights and warm days."

"Yes, ma'am," Miles acknowledged her announcement of the first frost that year. He cocked his head toward the chimney and waited.

She took her own comfortable time before she said, "Ol' Miss talk to me before I left from up there this mornin'."

The blanket flew aside as he skirted around the sheet.

"They gonna sell me, Mama Cee?" he asked in anguish.

"No," she chuckled, "Ol' Miss and I got what you call an understandin'. That's why you and me got plenty room in this cabin by ourselves. Ol' Miss stop anybody from lashing you, too. But you had no business up there actin' like you know what was in them books."

"What kind of understandin'? How 'bout Ol' Marse? What he say?" He shot his questions and eyed her nervously.

A blank look stole across her face. She began to hum the tune to a song that she sang to him when he was a child. It was a forbidden song on the plantation and she never allowed him to sing it for fear of the listening ears of the overseer. But now her humming filled the cabin. He moved his eyes to the floor and mouthed the words.

> Way down yonder in the middle of the field,
> Angels working at the chariot wheel.
> Not so p'ticular 'bout workin' at the wheel,
> Just want to see how the chariot feel.
> Let me fly,
> Now let me fly
> Way up to that kingdom, Lawd, Lawd.

"Son," she said as she began to lay more logs in the fire, "Ol' Marse say least you must be broke out of your bad ways 'fore you fit to live on his place again."

"What that mean?"

"That mean you going to the breakin' ground, some-where down in the next county, near the river."

"What that mean?"

"It mean they learn you how to behave when you come back here."

"When?"

"Tomorrow," she answered.

"In the morning . . . before you go up to the great house?" he asked, struggling to blot the tears out of his voice.

"I don't know," she answered lightly, like she was passing the time of day. "Ol' Miss didn't know her own self."

Miles searched her honey-brown face where wrinkles had drawn little pictures. Her gray eyes cut away from him again.

"Mama Cee," he started to ask. She went back to hum-ming her song.

Anger made his whole self shake as he paced the length of the small cabin and back again.

"Why this happenin' to me, Mama Cee . . . why don't us leave here when it get dark?" he said, feeling sick to his stomach with fear.

With one sweeping motion, Mama Cee pulled the sheet down.

"Put somethin' on your feet, son," she said without look-ing at him.

He started to the door for his shoes. A sharp pain halted his steps. Frowning at the rough floorboards, he eased him-self down to pull a splinter from beneath his big toe.

Mama Cee picked up his shoes and continued to scold gently when she saw that his foot did not bleed.

"You talkin' 'bout runnin'—that's foolish! Don't you know somebody watchin' us day an' night?"

Miles' chest caved in. He had not thought of that.

"You a smart boy and you ain't no runner," she said firmly, letting the heavy shoes fall to the floor. "Just don't go round messin' with them books no more when you come back here."

"Mama Cee," he pleaded, "I told you. I didn't go to know nothin' 'bout no books. Marse Gency mean as a dog— that's all to it!" For the tenth time he tried to explain. "The book fell open when I was wiping off the dust," his voice squeaked. "And one little picture caught my eye. I looked at it, that's all."

He could not explain the shiver that had run down his spine when he had heard someone sucking air and he had whirled around to see Gency Tillery's sixty-some-year-old, cold blue eyes staring at him from the parlor archway.

"Marse Gency, sir," Miles had tried to acknowledge the master's presence.

Without a word, Gency Tillery had walked swiftly to the heavily draped window and pulled the bell cord that summoned Macon. Gency Tillery spoke to his servants-in-training through the people who trained them.

Mama Cee went on, trying to keep Miles talking.

"You know Marse Gency say a book-learned servant is

dissatisfied. He don't want no dissatisfied servant 'round him and his family."

"You ever seen inside a book, Mama Cee?" Miles asked gently.

"No," she answered.

They stared at the blazing fire crackling up the chimney. A little picture of a white man with a jutting jaw and ruffles at his neck pulled at Miles' memory. The peculiar inked lines and circles in the book had made no sense to him.

After Mama Cee left to help out in the nursery, he ate a little from the skillet of sweet potatoes and fried meat skins she had left in the warm coals. Then he fixed himself to wait behind the closed door until tomorrow like Mama Cee said. Until the day before, he had thought only of the day he was living. Now the early days of his childhood crept before him.

Mama Cee was there, telling him in her singsongy voice, "You had a whole mouth o' teeth when Ol' Miss give you to me. They could see right off you was smart."

Even though they lived separately after Miles was chosen for the great house, Macon let him visit her a few times each month. During his visits, usually on Sunday, Mama Cee did not mind wrapping her arms around him and crushing him against her in front of the others.

"See how big my boy growing."

The grown folks made over him good-naturedly. The young boys and girls around his age giggled at his shamed face. Some of them fingered his starched white shirt and knee britches like they were made of precious gold.

As the hours passed, Miles sometimes laughed at his thoughts. Sometimes he frowned. Sometimes he dreamed of running free like a deer he had seen leaping at the edge of the wood. The sunlight splashed through the cracks of the outside wall and onto the floor. No clock struck to mark the hours of the day like at the great house. Miles could count to twelve. That was all. The servants-in-training polished the clock and washed its dirty face, but they dared not look too long at the numbers.

He had always smiled like he was supposed to when he opened the heavy brass-handled doors to Gency Tillery's grandchildren. He did not complain when the children wanted to ride his back like he was a horse. The other servants-in-training smiled too.

"I want to ride Miles' back this time," he remembered one little boy shouting excitedly. "Bend down, Miles, so I can ride."

Miles pushed the little boy's voice to the corner of his mind. Except for the sound of small children crying, until one of the old women hushed them, the rows of cabins were quiet. That morning took its time.

Finally afternoon and evening wore down to Mama Cee walking through the cabin door. He wanted to run and hug her, but fear held him back. He wanted to tell her how alone he felt.

"How you getting on, son?" she asked sadly.

He curled his lips into a smile and answered, "Fine, Mama Cee, real fine."

A long time after nightfall, Miles heard field hands tap at the cabin door, away from the overseer's ears. Obviously, they had heard about the breaking ground too.

"Miss Cee," they whispered, one after the other, "just want you to know I'm mighty sorry 'bout your trouble."

"Hold on 'til a change come."

"Tell dat boy to be strong."

"Nothing don't last always."

"Dat boy gonna make it."

Mama Cee accepted each one with a gracious, "Much obliged, certainly so, I thank you all."

By the time the tapping stopped Miles understood the fear Mama Cee had been trying to hide. Something more terrible than he could imagine was about to happen to him; there was nothing he could do.

"I love you, Miles," Mama Cee said to him from the other side of the sheet. Miles tucked the heels of his hands under his chin and squeezed his eyes together. No one had ever said that to him. Not even Mama Cee. Yet, he knew what it meant. He opened his mouth to say the same to her. Only a puff of air came out.

The rustling corn shuck mattress gave in to her weight. Soon he heard her light breathing even out to deep sleep. Something closed the door to his wakefulness.

# Chapter 2

A soft scrapple of sound startled Miles out of sleep. Even so, he kept still. The creaking floorboards let him know that halting footsteps were coming nearer. He sprang up and backed away from his pallet. Something or someone moved between him and the only door of the cabin.

"Mama Cee!" he yelled in the direction of the hanging sheet, hoping she would answer.

"Move easy, Miles—move easy, boy," Bounty's raspy voice said. "Time you be comin' out to the wagon wid me, now."

"Mama Cee!" Miles cried her name again.

Surprisingly, the old man moved quickly through the darkness and clapped a hand over Miles' mouth. The other hand clamped around the boy's neck.

"Cee at the big house," Bounty rasped quietly. "This ain't no time to say bye-bye. Marse Gency say he don't want no weepin' and wailin' 'round heah."

Miles' body stopped struggling. He felt the cold shackles clamp around his thin ankles. Bounty turned the key to lock them in place. The weight of them slowed him down as the old man led him down the path, well beyond the slaves' quarters. A mule-drawn wagon was waiting. With Bounty's help he half-slid and half-climbed aboard the hard seat.

"I don't care 'bout myself," Miles pleaded desperately to Bounty from his side of the buckboard. "I just want to say one little thing to Mama Cee before we go. We won't make a fuss."

Bounty stopped coiling the reins around his gnarled hands and mimicked, "What is dat one lil' thing?"

"I want to tell her I love her, that's all," Miles said softly.

The old man's laugh broke out of his chest like a gust of wind.

"Love!?" he wheezed out. "Ain't no such thing for us, boy. Love? Huh! Who put a notion like dat in yo' head?"

Miles stared off, realizing that he had made a mistake.

Bounty lashed at the mule. The buckboard lurched forward. The old man held the reins tight for balance and lashed at the mule again. Miles shivered and clung to the side of the seat, trying not to bump against Bounty's bony frame.

Soon the wobbly wheels bounced along the edge of the cotton fields and onto a red dirt road. This road led away from Tillery to the east. Miles remembered that Macon had let him ride muleback on a part of this road to the Jemison Plantation, about a year ago. They would be passing there soon. That was the first time he had ever left the Tillery Plantation. Now he was leaving for the second time and he didn't know if he would ever return.

The first bell tolled. He dared to look back. The white

16

gables of the great house poked up through a thin mist in the moonlight. That was the last he saw of it.

"Well, boy," Bounty said with a snicker still in his voice, "sun be up nigh. Ye be there 'fore sunset. Yassar. Travelin' on de Long-Ways Road, boy."

Miles kept his head down and his mouth clamped shut. Sunrise wore into a warm midmorning. They passed three plantations with sandy driveways lined with towering oak trees like at the Tillery Plantation. The driveways led to mansions that perched on hills so folks could see how rich they looked. None of them looked as rich as Gency Tillery's great house. Miles craned his neck, trying to get a good view of the stately carriage houses and coaches. He could not see the servants' cabins nor the stables. He guessed that such buildings would be hidden from the road as at Gency Tillery's place.

"Bounty, where this place they call the breakin' ground?" he took a chance to ask.

"Still a right smart piece from here, boy," Bounty answered eagerly. "They call it Wettown, I believe. Been a great while since I been dere."

"Sound like it's near water," Miles said, not mentioning that Mama Cee had told him about a river.

"You right, boy," Bounty confirmed, giving Miles a respectful glance. The buckboard seat grew quiet again.

The mule plodded slowly along the Long-Ways Road, as Bounty called it. Miles had heard Macon call it "the road to Tillery" or "the road to the Jemison Plantation."

Before long the old man pulled the mule over to the side to make room for two wagonloads of jostling field hands. Their pity leaped out to Miles in knowing looks. Some of them spat on the ground after they looked at the old man, but Bounty acted like he didn't see them. Miles wondered if Bounty had tracked any of them.

A big red stallion galloped toward them with a white man in a fancy gray riding habit on its back. He pulled up on the reins and tipped his hat to Bounty like he knew him. Bounty fumbled at the brim of his raggedy straw hat. Miles felt the man's glare even though their eyes did not meet. The man cropped his horse on the rump.

Miles squinted and shaded his eyes from the hot noonday sun for a while. Then his stomach began to growl. He was thirsty. Bounty had said nothing about food or drink. A while back he did notice a burlap bag crumpled under Bounty's side of the seat.

Suddenly, the mule stopped in the middle of the road and shook its head up and down. Miles looked from the mule to Bounty's grin. The slack reins lay across the old man's lap.

The mule made a sharp turn to the right and bounced them across the uneven ground to what looked like grazing land. A pear tree was just ahead. Miles watched the mule stop here and there to chomp on the tender blades of grass and clover.

"That mule know how to kill hungry, boy," Bounty said, pointing at the grass. "How 'bout you?"

Forgetting his shackles, Miles rose, kicking and hitting at Bounty.

"I ain't no mule and I ain't low like no mule. Don't you call me 'boy' no more. You know my name is Miles! Miles!" he screamed, startled at his own voice.

Surprised, Bounty caught the flailing fists and held on to keep from falling over the side.

"Leave go of me!" Miles yelled in the old man's face, spraying specks of slobber. They yanked back and forth with Bounty being the stronger. Neither of them noticed that the mule had stopped to bite at the sweet, autumn pears. Finally, the old man opened his own fists and Miles fell back. The boy hung his head and cried for a minute.

"Ye won't put a stop on me money—ye heer me?" Bounty threatened.

"What money?" Miles asked, still shaky but curious at the same time.

"Money I git fa taking ye ta de breakin' ground."

"Marse Gency give you money . . . for taking me—?"

"Uh-huh," Bounty cut in, his face growing a slight smile.

"What you do with the money?" Miles asked, wiping his face on his sleeve.

"Dat's me bizness. Nobody know me bizness."

"I know your business," Miles wanted to scream at Bounty. "Your business is mean." He watched Bounty's puzzling smile grow wider. Not caring anymore, the boy eyed the mouth-watering pears hanging from the tree. Before he knew it, Bounty pressed a tied-up bandanna against his chest. The tasty smell of cheese and molasses curled around his nose.

"Eat," Bounty ordered, smile gone. "Us git a drink of water at dat spring. It got ta be 'round here somewhar."

With trembling hands, Miles untied the knots and separated the four corners of the bandanna one at a time, ignoring the sound of Bounty's impatient sighs.

"Eat," Bounty ordered again. "Us ain't half there."

The meal of three thick corn pones, soaked in molasses, and the hunk of cheese tasted as good as it smelled. They ate. Miles had eaten two pones before his hands ceased to tremble. Bounty finished first and threw his bandanna under the buckboard seat.

"Dem pones taste good," he said, wiping his hand on his britches. He watched Miles take his last few bites before he bragged, "I stole de cheese when Cook turn't her head."

"Mama Cee say stealin' is wrong," Miles blurted out. Then his mind's picture of Mama Cee reminded him that he had not said good-bye to her. He stared into the shimmering heat waves, remembering.

"What ye lookin' at?" Bounty prodded.

"Nothin'," Miles said.

Bounty grunted and helped him off the buckboard. Miles hobbled a few short steps and flopped in the shade of the pear tree, rubbing his ankles. He could sense Bounty's eyes on him. His own eyes followed the mule as it pulled the buckboard around to the other side of the tree where ripe fruit bent the limbs lower to the ground. The mule kept crunching. Miles closed his eyes. He almost jumped out of his skin when Bounty grabbed his ankles.

Bounty laughed and yelled, "Hold still, 'til I unloose dese heah chains. Bring yo'self to the spring wid me. Den ye go 'hind the bushes an' take keer yo' bizness. 'Member if ye don't come back, ye nebber lay your lil' eyes on Mama Cee no mo'. When dem breakers get done wid ye...."

"What breakers do?" Miles asked, frightened, forgetting about the water.

Bounty trudged ahead, lifting his short legs above the tall grass. The look of the old man's stiff back told Miles that Bounty had the upper hand.

Cool spring water bubbled out of the white, sandy earth. Miles dropped to his knees and cupped handfuls to drink. Then he splashed his face and head. When he returned from the bushes Bounty was under the tree, re-rolling the legs of his too-long britches. Water dripping from the mule's mouth let him know that Bounty had let the animal drink too. The shackles were nowhere to be seen.

"Pull some dem pears an' throw 'em in de back," Bounty said, climbing onto the buckboard.

Miles hesitated.

Bounty turned, frowned at the boy, and said, "Ain't stealing. Dis land 'longs to Marse Gency's brother. Him know me."

That anyone as mean as Marse Gency had a brother was a surprise to Miles. No one at the great house had ever mentioned a brother. He looked around and quickly pulled seven or eight low-hanging pears. Then he ran freely and jumped onto his side of the seat. The pears tumbled between his knees. He turned and watched the fruit roll to the back of the wagon where Bounty had thrown the shackles.

"Git me dem shackles," Bounty ordered, not turning around.

A wounded sound escaped the boy's throat.

"Can't let folks see me wid you w'out shackles," Bounty said.

While Bounty tugged at his ankles, Miles wanted to kick the old man upside the head and run. Fear made him sit there and feel like he had been cut in two. One half blamed himself for his troubles. The other half blamed his love for Mama Cee. He could never run away from her. She was his only family now. Somewhere on the Long-Ways Road, he had given up his servant-in-training family.

In no time he heard the familiar click around his ankles. Bounty turned the screw on the shackles.

"Git up dere, mule," Bounty yelled.

Soon the narrow road stretched between straight-up pines. The wagon wheels bumped along on the hard dirt.

Miles rocked his body to the rhythm of the bumps. *Mama Cee, breaking ground, Mama Cee, breaking ground* pounded in his head every time the wheels turned over.

"What ails you?" Bounty squeezed out.

"Nothin' ails me," Miles stopped to answer, trying to keep the image of Mama Cee out of his mind. He went back to rocking, but not as much as before.

By the time the sun was about three hours behind them, most of the pears had been eaten. Then Miles was surprised to hear Bounty say "Gee!" The mule obeyed and turned right to stop not far away at a ramshackle building with a shed. Two young mules and an old workhorse drank from a trough in a fenced stable yard.

Miles did not know what to think of the blazing fire pit until a red-faced man with freckles dipped a glowing horseshoe into a tub of sizzling water. "Blacksmithing," the boy thought to himself.

"Well now! Get yerself down, Bounty," the sweating man invited. His round belly and flopping white hair were of no interest to Miles. He knew that he was not to speak or leave the wagon. He listened to their words.

"On your way to the breaking ground, are you?" the sweating man asked, glancing at Miles.

"Yassar, Mist' Mac, need me a fresh mule too. I'ma hard-time driver," Bounty bragged as he scooted over the marshy ground and made his way to meet the man.

"Why don't you give up this dreadful business, man? I

did, and glad of it," Mac said, shaking his head from side to side. "Getting too old, aren't you?"

Miles closed his ears to their passing the time of day until the white man turned his attention away from Bounty and walked toward the wagon. The boy raised up, sat on his hands, and dropped his head to ward off the pity directed to him. He couldn't figure out why he didn't want anyone to feel sorry for him. His eyes began to sting.

"How old is he?" Mac yelled over his shoulder, putting sympathy in his tone of voice.

"He ol' 'nough," Bounty answered loudly. "Help me ketch dis mule!"

Miles was glad to see the man rush to the stable to help corner the rearing beast.

When the new mule pulled the wagon onto the road, Miles looked back a part of the Long-Ways Road that they had traveled. The road appeared to be crooked, with a slight rise. He guessed that they were going downhill.

"Let's see heer," Bounty said to himself, yanking on a small pocket watch that dangled on the end of a rusty chain.

"He can tell time," Miles thought, his heart racing. He leaned toward Bounty to get a better view of the small face.

Wordless, the old man crammed the watch into a small pocket that Miles had not noticed until now.

"What time the clock say, Mister Bounty?" Miles dared to ask.

"It say time ta mind yo' bizness," Bounty answered.

They rode on and on without speaking. The hot sun had passed over them when Bounty looked to the left and pointed out, "Sun sinking—look at dem tree shadows. Dey be getting long-o, us be dere nigh."

Miles was heartened because Bounty had a kinder tone in his voice. But the old man's way of talking struck him as being funny for the first time that day. He smiled to himself and thought, "If folks talked like that in the great house, Mrs. Bethenia or Macon would fuss 'em out." Especially Mrs. Bethenia with her, "Don't you talk like a field hand or some Afrikun in this house." She would say, "You're a servant."

Again, he started to ask Bounty about the breaking ground, but he didn't know if the words would come out of his mouth right. After twisting and turning, he heard his own shaky voice ask, "Mister Bounty, Marse Gency ever send you to the breakin' ground?"

"Naw."

"Oh."

"I ain't nebber been on de block neither," Bounty said, offering a little more about himself.

"Block?"

Bounty gazed at Miles.

"Ye ain't nebber seen nothin' in yo' lil' life," he scoffed.

Miles agreed by shaking his head, hoping the conversation would come around to the breaking ground.

Bounty took a deep breath and quickly threw out, "If ye

a slave an' dey make ye stand on de block, ye waits for white folks ta say how much dey buy ye for. Den ye go wid dem 'cause dey pay for ye—see?"

Miles nodded his head. That meant being sold off. "Jest like me," the boy thought, closing his eyes and thinking, "Macon and Mrs. Bethenia say we servants 'cause it sound good, but we slaves." If only he could find out about the breaking ground. "Must be a terrible place," he thought, remembering Mister Mac's pity-eyes.

The new mule took to the Long-Ways Road the same as the old one. The flat lay of the land made his work easy. The mule kept picking four feet up and putting four feet down. That was all he had to do. They joined the cool of the evening that met them in the fork of the Long-Ways Road.

A glance at the old man's balled-up lips and stiff neck told the boy not to ask any more questions about the breaking ground.

Miles stretched his torso to reach the last pear where it rested at the other end of the wagon bed. He could see Bounty did not care so he bit into the juicy sweetness and hummed a tune he had heard the field hands sing.

For a little while, the sun suspended like a ball of fire over the tall pines in the west. Then its brightness dropped out of sight. Miles knew it was a foolish wish, but he wished that the red streaks the sun had painted on the sky would last forever.

Soon the wagon wheels were running smoothly over a road laid in bricks. The pattern of bricks passed under the wheels at a dizzying speed. New sounds and smells filled the air. "This must be Wettown," he thought, trying to find a dividing line between the narrow, close-together buildings that seemed to shoot up out of the ground. He had never been to a town before. Lanterns, not yet lit, hung from every post.

Black and white faces, young and old, laughed and smiled. He noticed that the black faces belonged to bodies that carried large, covered baskets on their heads and lifted or rolled barrels down the pattern of bricks.

The white faces belonged to bodies that walked about on the hard surface in cutaway coats and fine frocks and velvet capes. Never had he seen so many white men and women and flaxen-haired children in one place. The number of white faces would have struck fear into him were they not happily bowing and waving handkerchiefs to each other.

"White folks git ready ta ball dance, I reckon," Bounty figured out loud.

Shiny carriages rode by, dark-skinned drivers perched high in silk and wool livery. Their leather whips flicked lightly over big shiny horses.

"Well, looky." Bounty nodded his head toward the carriage drivers. "Ye want ta be up dere in a high-o seat?" he asked with merriment in his voice.

"They still slaves," Miles breathed to himself as he

watched how proudly their derbies were pulled to the side of their heads.

Suddenly, he jumped straight up and whirled around to find the cause of an earsplitting noise.

Bounty snickered at the boy's ignorance and pointed out, "Dat de train whistle. It b'hind dat depot."

He had heard tell that the little town of Tillery had trains but he had never seen one. He gawked at the red brick building, hoping to catch sight of the whistle at least. Not wanting Bounty to laugh at him, he kept his questions to himself.

After that the road turned to dirt again and ran along a narrow river. Miles searched for the last few shadows the sun had left behind. The wind was calm. He closed his eyes and let the force of the wagon's movement lull him into thinking—about Bounty.

The boy felt like his mind could be eased some if Bounty would only take a message back to Mama Cee. The spiteful-acting Bounty was not much to hope for in a friend, but the old man would leave him soon. Then he would be left alone to grapple with the breaking ground.

"I ain't gonna cry," he thought. Tears began to drip beneath his eyelids.

"Ye ailing?" Bounty asked, annoyed.

"I ain't ailing," Miles said. "Mister Bounty, I'm scared." Now he had shamed himself out loud.

"Ye be awright sho' as your name, Miles."

"What did you say?" Miles asked, not believing his ears, not knowing why he felt a tad of comfort.

"Ye heered me, Miles." Bounty softened his tone again.

The boy's lips moved up and down but no sound of a message to Mama Cee came forward. Maybe the old man would turn on him as quick as a heartbeat like before. Miles' eyes closed again, glad that there was no more for him to see.

# Chapter 3

After the sun's shadows completely disappeared to the west, Bounty hollered out, "Whoa, mule!"

Miles flung open his eyes. The mule had stopped several feet in front of a huge red barn. He could make out two small clapboard houses in the distance. Horses neighed in a stable nearby.

"Whoa, mule!" Bounty hollered again, taking his voice up another notch.

Two men carrying lanterns emerged from behind a barn door that was big enough for two wagons to pass through side by side. Miles could not make out the features in their white faces. He judged their height by the way they carried the lanterns.

"State your business," the taller one spoke through his nose. At once, both men raised their lanterns and neared the wagon like they expected something to jump out at them. The light showed the shorter of the two press his right hand on his sidearm.

"They must be breakers," Miles thought. He wondered if Bounty had seen the gun.

"State your business," the taller one said again with more urgency.

"Name Bounty, under Marse Gency Tillery's orders," the old man said like he had been practicing what to say for a long time. "Dis bad slave heah gots ta stay wid y'all 'cording ta dese papers."

Miles caught a fleeting glimpse as the tall one snatched the papers out of Bounty's hand. Miles held his breath and waited for Bounty to grow mean and short in his funny way of talking. Bounty sat in place, silent.

The tall one studied the papers by the lantern light and stuffed them into his pocket.

Miles' breath quickened when the shorter of the two sidestepped to him. Suddenly, the man yanked hard on the shackles. Miles tried to lessen the pain by moving his legs within closer reach without kicking the man. He was afraid to cry out.

"Gimme the key to these shackles," the short one said coldly.

Bounty quickly dropped the reins and patted the outside of his patched pockets. He anxiously searched one pocket, then the other. The two men sucked their teeth as a clump of unraveled twine, two smooth flint rocks for starting a fire, and a twisted wire fell from Bounty's hands. Finally, a hand shot up from where he had found the key in the folds of his rolled-up britches leg. The tall one snatched the key. Miles knew, now, that Bounty was not going to turn mean.

"Get down from there," the short one ordered after

unlocking the shackles. Miles jumped to the ground.

"Get in there," the tall one said, pointing to the wide-open barn door.

When Miles got within a few feet of the door, Bounty's voice returned. Miles was astonished to hear the old man laugh heartily and spout, "Yassar, gent'men, Ol' Bounty be on the Long-Ways Road 'fore sunup. Yassar."

Miles squinted through the crack in the door to see Bounty standing atop the wagon seat in the dim light, prancing up and down and singing at the top of his voice.

> *Tell Cee 'bout my troubles,*
> *Tell Cee 'bout my troubles,*
> *One o' dese days.*
> *Gonna tell Cee um all right,*
> *Gonna tell Cee um all right,*
> *When I git home.*

The two men were mocking him and swaying their lanterns to the beat of the peculiar song.

"That's right, sing to us," one of them shouted.

But the young boy knew that the old man was singing to him and only to him. Bounty was going to let Mama Cee know that he was all right. Although the song did not exactly say anything about love, Miles knew Bounty was going to tell her that he loved her the best he could.

He watched Bounty take his seat again, out of breath.

"Git up dere, mule!" Bounty hollered, not as loud as before. The mule pulled out of the lantern light.

"Thank you, Mister Bounty," the young boy whispered to himself.

He wished he could have said it to Bounty. Then again, he felt that somehow Bounty knew. He turned around to face whatever there was in the barn.

The putrid odor of unwashed bodies reached out at him like clawing hands. He instinctively covered his nose and glanced around. The barn was awash in light from lanterns hung on the low-hanging girders and set about the sprawling floor. Even the loft was lit. From what he could see, about twenty or so black men were raised up on their elbows, staring at him from their pile-of-hay beds.

"Over here, you," another nasal voice rang out.

Miles pivoted to find the person that belonged to the voice.

"You see me, boy," the voice ordered. "Come over here."

The elbows collapsed in the corner of his eye as he approached the voice, somewhere in the dim section of the barn. A lantern was suddenly turned to its full light, catching the boy's eye. Two field mice scampered across the floor. Finally, Miles stood before one of the tallest, widest men he had ever seen. Muscles bulged through a collarless shirt. There seemed not a drop of fat on him. The man did not have his nose covered so Miles dropped his hand from his face and took short breaths. Silently, Miles took in the size of him. Then he gazed up toward the man's face at the butter-colored hair, eyes wide.

"Don't you look me in my face," the nasal voice warned between skinny lips. "Cast your black eyes down." The man leaned toward him.

Miles backed up and pointed to one of the girders just over the man's head.

"I ain't lookin' in your face," Miles said excitedly. "I was lookin' at that snake hangin' over your head."

The wide one snapped his bald head up. Sure enough, a moccasin snake, licking the air, was suspended from one of the girders. Within one instant three things happened. The elbows raised up. A shot rang out. Someone screamed. Miles caught his mouth, wondering if it was he who had screamed. A poisonous moccasin writhed at his feet among the strewn hay.

The slaves ran to every corner of the barn. Another shot rang out to stop them in their tracks.

"Get back to your places!" the short man from the barn-yard shouted, before anyone could reach the door.

The slaves crept back to their pile-of-hay beds. But Miles thought he heard a sprinkling of stifled snickers. He waited to be told what to do.

"Make your bed, boy," the wide man smirked, sweeping his hand toward the floor, nearer to the open doorway. A few yards away, another person lay turned away from the barn door.

Wearily, Miles walked to the spot and raked a pile of hay together with his hands. He lay down right away and kicked off his heavy shoes, looking up at nothing.

Suddenly, the wide man stood over him and demanded, "What they call you, boy?"

"Miles."

"Miles, what?"

The boy did not know how to answer this question.

"I see by these papers you belong to your master, Gency Tillery, so your name is Miles Tillery."

Miles had never heard "Tillery" tacked to his name.

"Mister Cobb is my name," the man said. "That's Mister Avery and that's Mister Burgess—he shot that snake."

Miles silently gave a glance to the short man named Avery. The tall thin one was Mister Burgess.

"You hear me, boy?"

"Yes, sir."

"I see here you've been a choice one too, haven't you?" Cobb said with menace in his voice, meaning that Miles had been favored and was deserving of punishment. Cobb pointed to the two other men and added, "Well, we're here to help choicey ones not to be so choicey."

The barn grew deathly quiet. Miles wondered if he should say, "Yes, sir," again.

Then shuffling footsteps neared the pile-of-hay bed. Slowly, the dead snake, looped around a hoe handle, extended over his chest. Try as he might, the boy could not look away to see who was holding the handle. Driblets of the snake's insides fell onto his shirt.

Cobb laughed.

"He 'longst to them rich Tillerys," one of the breakers stated as if Miles and the dripping snake did not exist. "Old family—whole town named for 'em."

It seemed that hours passed before they took the snake away and left him lying in his own sweat. Miles closed his eyes now, but he felt like his throat had shriveled. He did not move when someone rubbed the snake's innards from his shirt.

The barn doors creaked together and he became aware of snores and muffled voices and the awful odor around him. The boy had come to the end of one long journey.

"My name is Miles and I belong to Mama Cee," he breathed to himself before dropping off into a bottomless pit of sleep.

At the crack of dawn, the rustle of slaves scrambling to their feet startled Miles awake. He jumped to his feet too, and noticed that the barn door was open. One by one the slaves filed through the door to stand side by side in front of the same three men. They did not utter a word. Miles did not either. Miles was last in line on the damp ground.

Mister Cobb nodded his head down the line, counting each of them silently. Out of the corner of his eye Miles could see chins tucked down. Quickly, he dropped his head.

"Where is that Nero?" Cobb asked, alarmed. None of the slaves answered nor raised their heads.

The large man barged into the barn shouting, "Nero! Nero!" Avery tore out behind him.

Burgess ordered them all with his gun in the air, "Don't you move!"

The silent line stood in place.

Cobb and Avery returned within a few minutes without the one called Nero. Miles wondered who Nero was and where he had hidden or run off to. He strained to hear their quiet talk.

"He squeezed hisself through a hole he made in the side loft," one of them said.

"Yeah, he must've got out of the barn last night when all that snake ruckus went on," the other agreed.

"The dogs will take care of him first. Then we will show him how to run," Avery said viciously.

Miles sensed the threatening eyes on him. "They blame me," he thought.

He breathed easier when the bodies on each side of him began to twitch and shift from one foot to the other. They felt the tension too.

The smell of food pushed all else out of his mind. Abruptly, the slaves broke the line before he realized that one of the white men must have given a signal permitting the slaves to bolt in the direction of the cooking food. He ran to catch up.

"Ol' Nero ought to come back here jest to say, 'Thank you, sir,' to you, Miles," one man about Macon's age grinned out after he waited for Miles to catch up. "My name Elijah, Miles—how you be?"

"All right, I reckon," Miles said, not knowing what else to say.

They trotted on to the open shed, but the others had already beaten them to the pile of wooden bowls and spoons. The men packed around the person who served the food, blocking him from sight.

At the same time, Miles and Elijah spotted two bowls facedown on the ground. Elijah grabbed them and used his sleeve to wipe the dirt away. He shoved one at Miles and squeezed his body among the crowd.

By the time Miles got the chance to reach out his bowl, the pot was empty except for a few sprigs of some kind of meat and a bit of brown liquid. The older man who scraped the bottom of the pot clicked his tongue and said, "You got to run faster. Ain't nobody feedin' no babies 'round here."

Miles could feel the rage and self-pity gurgle in his chest. He slammed his bowl onto the ground. Its scanty contents spattered. He stomped away amid laughter from the others. His anger and hunger sapped every bit of his strength.

"Hey, you!" Mister Cobb yelled to him.

"Yes, sir?" he answered meekly.

Cobb half smiled and beckoned with his head. Miles

stumbled over to him, expecting to be told where to find food.

From nowhere, Cobb's beefy hand shot out and slapped him onto the ground.

"That'll teach you not to waste food here!"

Miles heard the words mix with ringing bells. The young boy felt no pain, but his head roared like there had been a clap of thunder. He lay on the ground, wondering how he could make the noise go away. Slowly it did, but he had passed out.

"Wake up, dere, Miles," Elijah said and shook him urgently. Miles shivered and hugged himself to a sitting position. The sun was about an hour high. He felt soaked to the bone.

"Dey be puttin' so much water on you 'cause you wouldn't come to," Elijah explained.

"Mama Cee," Miles moaned.

"Don't you be callin' on nobody 'round here. Don't you know where you be?" Elijah asked and pulled Miles to his feet.

"Um at the breakin' ground," Miles slurred, trying to straighten his muddled thoughts. He wanted to ask what had happened to him, but he was too tired to say more.

Somehow Miles found himself on a pile of hay in the barn. Barely, he lifted his hand to touch the left side of a swollen face that throbbed like it had a heart of its own. Each throb sent shooting pains across his skull. No matter how many times he blinked his eyes, the barn's loft seemed to soar as high as the sky, then topple to his chest, causing him to jump.

Elijah loomed over him with an open jar.

"Drink this," he offered, dropping to his knees and holding the young boy's head up.

The sharp smell of molasses water stirred Miles' hunger. He gulped, ignoring the throbbing pain until Elijah pulled the jar to the side and let it lean against the hay. When Miles tried to say "thank you," Elijah poked a piece of corn bread between his swollen lips.

"Don't try to chew," he cautioned when Miles flinched. "Jest let it get soft 'fore you swallow."

About ten minutes passed before the last of the molasses water and bread painfully disappeared. Then Elijah eased him down and covered his body with hay from head to toe. Warmth from the hay gave him some comfort. The throbbing in his head eased some too. He peeped up through the shards of hay at the loft. It stayed in its place.

Images of the empty pot and the laughing slaves formed in his mind. Cobb's image was the last to return, but he could not recall the lick he took upside his head.

"I'm better now," Miles said weakly.

"You stay better all de time if you don't show nobody how you feel," Elijah said with a smile on his face. "You can't survive de way you goin', little man," he added solemnly.

"I was so hungry," Miles said, excusing his anger. "Y'all didn't save me nothin' hardly to eat—and y'all just like me."

Miles saw Elijah sweep his head from side to side, astonished at the excuse. He paced out of Miles' eyesight and back again. Finally, he spoke.

"Miles, if Cobb had killed you on your first day here, he would've had to pay your master full price for you. That's why you are not dead. That's why he told me to stay with you for a while and feed you."

The talk of death frightened Miles. He believed what Elijah said about Cobb, but he could not believe the way Elijah talked, like a rich man, standing tall. The field-hand talk was nowhere to be heard.

Miles brushed some of the hay from his face so he could see the words glide out of Elijah's mouth. Elijah noticed the boy's staring eyes and continued.

"You were sent here to have your spirit broken so you will forever believe that you are a slave. The breakers will do anything, short of killing you, to break your spirit. Don't make such a hullaballoo every time something does not suit you. You must learn to hide your true feelings and bide your time. Do you understand?" Elijah asked as he stepped back quietly.

Miles looked at a corner of the barn. He understood, but he had to remake Elijah's words to fit his own thoughts. Elijah talked about spirit, his spirit. Even though Elijah did not say so, Miles knew within himself that a broken spirit was just as bad as death. Now this man was telling him to hide his feelings so he could save his spirit.

Painfully, he thought about the dripping snake hanging

41

over his chest the night before. He wanted to ask Elijah how he could have hidden his true feelings that time, but he did not. "Got to fix my own spirit, somehow," he thought to himself.

"Do you understand or need I expound further?" Elijah asked.

"I understand," Miles answered quickly, remembering how "expound" looked when it glided out of Elijah's mouth and thinking, "He know 'bout books."

The young boy looked into Elijah's eyes and dared to say, "I want to know 'bout books."

"Hush!" Elijah hissed, looking toward the barn door.

Miles stiffened. He let his hand fall as shuffling steps neared them faster than he thought possible.

"Did he come to?" Cobb asked, looking at Miles' closed eyes.

"Yassar, Mist' Cobb," Elijah answered with a grin in his tone. "He be ready for to work 'fore long."

"Open your eyes, boy," Cobb ordered, ignoring Elijah.

Miles opened his eyes and put a little smile on his face. Cobb was satisfied.

"In one hour I want you ready for work, you hear me?"

"Yassar," Miles answered, looking in another direction.

Cobb twisted his thick neck around to Elijah. Miles was surprised at the fear Elijah painted all over his dark brown face as he looked at the floor.

"Elijah!" Cobb yelled suddenly. Elijah jumped.

Cobb sealed his lips against clenched, yellow teeth. His balled-up fist moved like he was going to strike Elijah.

Elijah stepped to the side.

Miles was intent on watching Elijah change his body movements and the muscles in his face to fool Cobb.

"Take your trifling, black self back to work," Cobb strained out. "I'll tell you when to come and get this little ugly buzzard."

Elijah turned on his heels and ran out of the barn.

Without looking back, Cobb walked out of the barn.

Miles took a deep breath and went back to thinking and asking himself questions. Where did Elijah come from? Was he a servant in a great house too? Maybe not, because Elijah used words he had never heard from Mrs. Bethenia or Macon.

He was sure that no further harm had come to him because he had hidden his true feelings from Cobb. He had to bide his time like Elijah said.

# Chapter 4

Faintly, the wind blew sounds of deep singing voices and grunts into the drafty barn. Miles was reminded of the field hands that he had heard singing in the distance on the Tillery Plantation. Cobb did not say anything about the kind of work the slaves were doing. He wished he had asked Elijah.

His eyes followed the buzzing deer flies zigzagging across the barn. His head began to ache again. He patted his puffy face. It hurt. He tried to push his body into a sitting position. His head hurt more. He lay back down and drifted in and out of sleep.

He awoke with Elijah brushing the hay to the side. Miles sat up and looked around for Cobb.

"It's just me," Elijah said. "Time for you to work."

Miles blurted while he had the chance, "Do you know 'bout books, Elijah?"

"If you mean can I read, yes," Elijah said with a curious smile on his face.

"He know I won't tell. Maybe he can learn me," Miles thought with quiet gladness. "That's what I want to do, read books," his mind raced.

"Let me tie this rag around your head, tight," Elijah requested, steadying the crown of Miles' head with his long fingers. "Ease the pain," he added kindly.

The tight rag did squeeze some of the pain away.

"Can you learn me to read books?" Miles questioned. He had been trying to ask for the last minute or so.

"I have no books here," Elijah said, peeling a boiled sweet potato.

Miles felt foolish and ashamed that he had not thought of that. The breaking ground rules were the same as on the Tillery Plantation. No slave was allowed to read. He stood up and limped toward the gaping door, paying no attention to the sweet potato.

"I can teach you to read without books," Elijah said.

"How?" Miles asked, rushing back as fast as his throbbing head let him.

Elijah hushed him by talking in whispers.

"You must learn the letters first. Then the words." Seeing the confused look on Miles' face, he added quickly, "What is the shortest breaker's name?"

"Mister Avery," Miles said, still confused.

"A, Avery," Elijah said clearly. "His name starts with the letter A. Say it."

"A," Miles said eagerly.

"Who killed the snake?" Elijah asked.

"Mister Burgess," Miles said, nodding his head for Elijah to continue.

"B, Burgess. Say it."

45

"A, B," Miles said to show Elijah he had not forgotten the first letter. "Cobb is next," he spouted. "He is the biggest."

"Cobb, C. Say it."

"C," Miles said. "A, B, C."

"Now you know what the first three letters sound like. I'll teach you what they look like."

"When?"

"When the time is right," Elijah's voice cautioned. "Don't tell a soul."

Miles shook his head from side to side. He would rather die than tell.

"Come on," Elijah urged in slave talk. "Dey be lookin' for us 'fore long. Eat piece of dis tater."

Miles bit into the soft potato. Right then, he decided he was going to use field-hand talk the same as Elijah.

He felt like he was stepping up on air as he followed Elijah around the smokehouse and food shed. They stopped to get a drink from the well. Then there were the stables he had not been able to see the night before or that morning. Near the two clapboard houses, a pen of dogs growled and fought over a ham bone like they were going to chew on each other instead of the bone.

Pretty soon, they made their way across a spongy field of freshly cut hay. Miles heard chopping axes mix with singing voices coming from the skirt of woods. In the distance, a spiraling pine tree bowed and crashed amid celebrating shouts.

"Dey cuttin' down trees," Miles said to Elijah's back like Elijah didn't already know.

"I reckon dey gonna make you a trimmer," Elijah said, slowing down. "You ever cut wood?"

"I be a servant-in-trainin' at the great house," Miles said. Elijah snickered good-naturedly.

"I be able to tell dat by de looks of you. You ain't never lifted nothin' no bigg'n a spoon."

Another treetop vanished from sight.

"I ain't scared," Miles said.

"Don't follow me," Elijah warned suddenly, and forked away from the straight path.

Miles understood when he spotted Cobb waving from the edge of the woods. He tried to quicken his steps without jarring his head. Beads of sweat burst and ran down his back.

"Don't let me have to show you how not to trifle away your time," Cobb yelled when Miles reached the edge of the woods. Miles thought it best to keep his mouth shut and his head down while he stood so close to Cobb.

"No need for you to worry 'bout him," a new voice came out of the woods. "They got the hardest heads in the world, like baboons."

"Beat 'em side the head all day and it won't kill 'em," another new voice said. Taunting laughter broke out among them.

"Sometimes it take a beating on the head to break 'em."

Miles jerked his head up. Three white men that he had not seen before were staring at him. He cast his eyes to the ground again and wondered if Elijah knew what letter their names started with. With a smile in his heart, he thought that if they knew of the three letters he had hidden in his head they would surely beat them out. Gency Tillery would be glad to pay them to do just that, too.

Cobb pointed and ordered harshly, "Pick up that axe, boy."

Miles went over and tugged on the handle of an axe someone had sliced into the soft dirt.

"Find Cookie," Cobb said, "and do like he tell you."

"C, Cookie," Miles thought.

The sidelong view of their folded arms told him they were waiting for him to behave like a baboon, whatever that was. He would ask Elijah when he got the chance.

The slaves' axes were hitting the mark between grunts and song when Miles stumbled out of the hot sun, through the underbrush, into the shady woods.

"They think I can't find Cookie," he whispered to himself, welcoming the coolness. He guessed that Cookie was the older man who had served the food earlier that morning.

That was the man he was searching for as he looked at all sizes and shapes of men who were chopping wedges of wood from the trunks of the tall pines. He shied away from the swinging axes, looking into the sweaty faces.

*"Timber!"* someone yelled.

Frightened, he turned around to see why the men were running past him at breakneck speed. In a flash, hands he did not see snatched his body, like a bunch of rags, out of the path of a tree an instant before it hit the ground, *"Wump!,"* like a dead animal.

Without delay, men shouted, "One mo' down!"

"All clear?" Cobb yelled the question.

"Yassar," several of the men yelled the answer, meaning a tree had not fallen on anyone.

Miles did not have to look further for Cookie. Cookie had found him and the axe that had fallen from his hand.

The slave men went on with their chopping and grunting and singing meaningless words while the white men surrounded them with guns and coiled whips.

> *If you gotta cook a possum, Huh!*
> *Cook him good and done, Huh!*
> *Lay him on a cooking rack, Huh!*
> *And hold him to the sun.*

Cookie led Miles deeper into the woods, to some pines that appeared to have been chopped down some time ago by the way the needles had turned yellow. One of the breakers stood nine or ten trees behind them.

In a little while Miles could hack off the soft pine limbs without jarring his head too much. Two other older men were hacking the limbs from a tree not far away. One of them looked as old as Bounty. What they had done to be sent to the breaking ground Miles could not imagine. He had not seen anyone near his own age.

"Water, water," a familiar voice called. Then Elijah emerged from behind a tree, lugging a bucket of water. Miles was surprised and glad to see his new friend even though Elijah took no notice of him.

"Water over heah," Cookie called back.

Elijah calmly dipped a gourd full of water for each of them. Miles hoped his own face looked as cool as the water that hit the bottom of his empty stomach.

"Water, water," Elijah trailed off, calling to the others.

Miles raised his axe higher and let it fall.

"We clearin' new ground for plantin' right now," Cookie told him, between hacks.

"Be a lot of firewood out here," Miles added to the conversation.

"Ain't no firewood—logs for breakers. Dey sell 'em," Cookie told him.

Miles learned through Cookie that some of the logs would be taken on wagons and loaded onto the freight train in Wettown where the whistle had scared him.

"De train got coaches and flatbeds," Cookie said knowingly. "Dey run 'long on tracks, see?"

Some would be floated down the Wettown River on something called a barge. Miles could not imagine the sight of a train or a barge no matter how many times Cookie described these things to him. He thought he had grown as dull-witted as Mrs. Bethenia said he would from sipping coffee.

So much had happened to him during the last few days; Miles was in a whirlwind of pain. Out of it all, three letters gave him the most courage.

"A, B, C," he practiced, silently, wishing Elijah had had the time to tell him more letters.

He looked up to see Cookie staring at him.

"I said," Cookie seemed to be repeating, "atta while I got to go cook for y'all. You go too and help out."

"Yassar," Miles said, trying not to show that he was pleased. His head had begun to throb again. He was afraid to stop long enough to retie the rag that kept slipping over his brow.

Finally, when the sun was almost down, Cookie told Miles to drag the limbs to a nearby bundle.

"We set fire to 'em atta while," he said. "We go cook now."

They followed the path to the shed. It was now exciting to hear the powerful singing and shouting echo from the woods. Miles looked back at the trees. One of the breakers was trailing them, not far behind. He looked back again when they stepped out of the hayfield and saw no sign of the breaker.

First off, Miles noticed that the dogs were no longer barking. Then he stared at the empty pen and tightened the rag around his head.

"Dey gone huntin'—huntin' for Nero," was all Cookie said.

Remembering the dogs' bristled hair and bared teeth, Miles did not want to trade places with Nero.

The cool of the evening had set in by the time the fire was lit under a large pot of water hanging near the shed. Cookie gave Miles the task of toting water from the well to fill a trough that was used for stirring cornmeal into something Cookie called cush. Cookie scooped the wet cornmeal, making little balls to drop into the pot of boiling salt pork, dried fish, wild onions, and turnips.

"Can I get my bowl and spoon, now?" Miles asked, trembling from hunger and eyeing the edge of the woods at the same time.

"Dey in the smokehouse—git mine too whilst you in dere," Cookie permitted, stirring the bubbling mixture with a long-handled gourd.

Miles gobbled down two bowls of the hot stew before the cook said, not unkindly, "No more. Other folks got to eat too."

Miles wanted to remind the cook that no one had thought to save anything for him to eat that morning, but thought it best to not make him mad. Cookie told him to set the bowls and spoons out and to cut kindling for the next morning.

The men ate, some of them not even looking to see what was in the bowl before they raked the food into their mouths with the spoon. Then they went to the well to drink gourds of water under the watchful eyes of the breakers. Everyone knew to stay within the circle of guns and whips. Sometimes the circle was as small as a ring game.

Cookie found any little thing for him to do while the breakers stood guard. Miles realized the cook was talking to protect himself.

"Rake dese ashes 'way, boy," Cookie ordered like he was talking to a small child. "And wash dese spoons and bowls —I got to lock de smokehouse—whar you at, boy?"

Like Cookie told him, Miles washed the coarsely hewn fixing table with smelly, homemade soap like that at Mama Cee's cabin.

A full moon hung over the trees when the men made their way to the barn. The light from the lanterns spilled out to wait for them. Cookie rushed ahead to claim his space.

Miles saw Elijah stoop to lace his shoe a few paces ahead.

"Gimme your hand," he stood up and whispered as Miles walked by.

Miles extended his right hand, wanting to know why Elijah was rubbing charcoal in his palm.

"Mister Avery be in the barn," he said, letting go of Miles' hand. "Remember him?"

"A," the boy thought to himself and looked at his hand. The moonlight showed him what looked like the form of a gable.

Elijah pushed him ahead into the lantern light. When Miles looked at his palm again he knew he was looking at the letter A. It reminded him of one of the gables on the great house with a line drawn through it. Quickly, he wiped his hand on his shirt until only a slight smudge remained. The letter's form was burned into his memory.

After all the lanterns except one were snuffed out, he lay on his pile-of-hay bed and drew imaginary A's on the ceiling, on the floor, and in the air. In his mind he fussed at himself because he had forgotten to ask Elijah about the word *baboon.* Then, without warning, it came to him that the word *baboon* had the same beginning sound as "Burgess!" he hollered and sprang up, making his head hurt.

Scuffling steps and a lantern rushed to his pile of hay. The breaker who held the lantern found Miles flat on his back. His eyes were closed. He snored quietly. The steps crept away.

Shortly after, real sleep turned him on his side.

For four or five days in a row, Elijah could not show Miles more new letters. By himself, the boy discovered the beginning sounds of his three precious letters all around him. Words like *apron, cat,* and *bag* reminded him that he would be ready for Elijah the next time. If only the next time would come.

One morning, about an hour before sunrise, Cookie poked Miles' stiff body awake to help ready the morning meal, as usual.

"How you be feelin', boy?" Cookie asked as they trudged

up to the shed. That was the first time the cook had asked after the boy's health.

"My head some better," Miles answered, not mentioning his sore muscles and regretting that he had not spoken to the older man first. Mama Cee would have fussed with him for not showing respect. "How you be, Mister Cookie?" he asked kindly, adding a handle to the name to make up for his ill manners.

He was almost moved to tears when Cookie paused before he said, "Jest call me 'Cookie' like the breakers say; I know you got a good heart in your body." As a second thought, Cookie answered, "Oh, I be fine, real fine."

By the time the breakers released the men from the counting line, Miles and Cookie had eaten their breakfast that contained the same ingredients as the many nights before. But it was just as tasty and hot, and it killed hunger. All of the men ate greedily with no complaints.

Pretty soon the breakers fanned out into a wide circle as the men entered the woods to begin felling trees. Miles and Cookie were dragging freshly cut limbs away from the logs when Avery ordered everyone back to the barn. The sun was barely an hour high.

"Dey found Nero, I bet," Cookie said, resting his axe against a log.

"What dey want wid us?" Miles asked as casually as he could.

"Dey got to show 'im off," Cookie said, shaking his head.

Cookie was scared and Miles didn't want to be in the company of a scared man. Elijah was not in sight yet, but he saw the breakers with guns drawn, their eyes flicking around, trying to see everyone at once. Even so, Miles spotted a few of the men swaggering over the fallen trees and kicking their way through the underbrush out of the woods.

"Dey tryin' to make out like dey ain't scared o' nothin'," Cookie said, drawing his shoulders around his neck.

"I ain't scared," Miles said to himself.

The breakers fell in line behind the men. They passed the pen that now held barking dogs.

"Thought maybe y'all wanted to see ol' Nero again," Cobb jeered as they gathered at the barn. Nero was strapped around a big maple tree with the side of his face ironed against the smooth bark. Nero's toes scarcely leveled the overgrown roots. By the looks of his naked back Miles could see that Nero was not much older than he was. A torn shirt lay crumpled at the base of the tree.

Cobb cracked the air with his whip.

"Have mercy on 'im," Cookie said to no one in particular.

Cobb gave him a "shut your mouth" stare.

Miles saw Elijah at the other end of the half circle of slaves. Since Elijah did not look in his direction, he decided not to move from his spot.

"Forty lashes," Avery said, flashing his hateful eyes and enjoying himself at the same time. "Who wants to lay on the first ten?"

To Miles' relief, no one moved. Avery's rabbity-looking

face reddened with excitement. "How 'bout you, Elijah?" Avery asked sternly.

"Naw sir," Elijah said jovially. "See, I got dis misery in my arm from totin' water." Elijah held his arms as if they had grown crooked.

The breakers bent double, laughing and slapping their thighs. Most of the half circle guffawed and bent their bodies double too.

Nero did not make a sound. Not even after Cobb laid on the first lash. After the third lash Nero still had not cried out or begged for mercy like Cobb wanted to hear. Something was very wrong.

The white men exchanged nervous glances before Cobb prodded Nero's neck with the butt of the whip. Nero's head bobbed like that of an old man falling asleep.

"He's dead," Avery said, disappointed.

"He scared to death," Cookie cried, not caring who heard him.

No one noticed when Miles' knees all but buckled.

"Take them straps off, Elijah!" Avery ordered.

Seven or eight men rushed in with Elijah to tear at the leather straps. Miles joined in, leaning against the rippling muscles of the others. Somehow his wobbly legs kept him upright. The breakers put guilty looks on their faces and widened the circle, ready to defend themselves.

"I got 'im," Elijah said with his arms around Nero's waist. "Y'all git back so I can ease 'im down."

Instead everyone surged forward, wanting to handle Nero.

Finally, they lowered the body onto the ground and folded the dead man's arms across his chest. Though he had heard of dying on Gency Tillery's plantation, Miles had never seen a dead person before. Nero looked like he was sleeping peacefully, except his chest didn't rise and fall.

He wished with all his heart that the moccasin snake had bitten Cobb that first night. Then Nero would be alive. Miles turned and looked into Cobb's face and the faces of the four other breakers. One breaker looked away rather than meet his gaze.

Cobb fired his gun at the sky and yelled, "Back to the woods, you brutes, lessen you want to lay down there with Nero!"

Without looking back, the men straggled in the direction of the woods with the breakers closing the circle.

"You, water boy," Cobb yelled from the rear.

Miles and Elijah stopped and looked back.

Cobb pointed with his gun barrel. "Bury him deep, over there, cross from the stables, under that persimmon tree."

"Yassar," Elijah said, heading back to the barn.

"Let that puny one what just come in here help you," Cobb fired off again as if Miles was not there.

"Yassar," Elijah said in the same lifeless tone. "Come on, Miles," he said loudly for Cobb to hear.

# Chapter 5

Miles reasoned that if he admitted to himself that he was afraid of Nero, then he would not dread digging the grave. When they wrapped the body with a gunnysack and dragged it to the persimmon tree, he realized that he was afraid of something else, not Nero.

"Mark my words," Elijah said, reaching for one of the shovels Miles had gotten from the tool shed. "The breakers are going to have to pay for this one."

"Cookie say Nero scared to death."

"Nero was never afraid of anything or anybody. By mishap he killed himself, but the breakers don't know it."

Miles eyed his friend as if suddenly he had been struck by some kind of craziness.

"Breakers wouldn't strap Nero to the tree if he was already dead," he argued.

Patiently, Elijah explained, "Nero stuffed his own mouth with a piece of his shirt. He was proud and didn't want us to hear him cry out. That first lick must have made him suck that rag down his throat. He choked to death."

Elijah sliced his shovel into the black dirt, outlining the shape of a grave.

"How you know that?" Miles asked in disbelief.

"I saw a string hanging from his chin as soon as he fell back. So I tucked it back in his mouth."

"I feel better now," Miles said, awed by what Elijah had told him.

"Why is that?"

"Because I thought Nero was scared like I was when they let that snake stuff fall on me. I thought I was gonna die 'cause I was scared. I'm still scared. But now I know Nero died 'cause he was proud."

"Before you start digging," Elijah said, scraping away dead grass with the shovel, "let me see you write the letter A in this dirt."

Miles got down on his knee and scratched A with his forefinger. He stood up for Elijah to approve. Elijah threw back his head and laughed.

It took them two hours to dig the grave and cover Nero's body with the red clay. Elijah shoveled dirt into a mound and marked the grave with a few small stones. During that time, Miles had learned the sound of ten letters. He could scratch the letters in the dirt too. Elijah paid no attention to the passing time. Miles began to worry.

Elijah noticed him jumping at the slightest noise.

"Those breakers are going to act as sweet as honey in a comb for a little while," he said.

"Why?" Miles asked, recalling with a shake of his head the excitement that stretched across the pale faces of the breakers when Nero was strapped against the whipping tree.

"Look at the circumstances from this point of view, Miles," Elijah requested like he was making a speech. "The breakers feel responsible even though they don't care that Nero died. Rest assured, they are not grieving. But what are they feeling?"

"I don't know——" Miles began.

"They feel at fault. A person that feels at fault expects what?"

Miles gave a helpless expression.

"Blame—punishment." Elijah punched his hand. "They feel blame for having destroyed someone's property. The punishment will be to pay full price to Nero's slaveholder."

"What that got to do with them actin' sweet and all?" Miles jumped back with a good argument. "They just pay for Nero—that's all."

Elijah paused and then broke into slave talk.

"De men be showin' signs—bad signs. Dey mought stir up trouble. Den slavers know dere's weakness on dese grounds."

Miles completed the picture, happy that he understood.

"Dey don't send nobody heah and breakers ain't got no logs for sellin'——"

"So dey po' on a lil' honey—distract de men," Elijah said. "Confuse 'em."

"And keep 'em workin'," Miles added.

"Den dey turn mean again," Elijah ended. "Just you wait and see."

Miles had so much to wait for. Knowing that he might not have the chance to talk to his friend again for some time, he tried to ask as many questions as he could. Elijah answered patiently.

"A baboon is an African monkey, an animal with a short tail and a dog-looking face."

He sketched into the soft dirt when Miles could not picture a train and a barge.

Miles piled one question on top of the other until he asked, "Where did you come from?"

"I was born in Johnson County, South Carolina, thirty-five years ago," Elijah answered shortly. Then he put a little smile on his face and added, soothingly, "One day I will tell you all about my family history, that is, all about me."

Miles figured the door to Elijah's past life was closed to him. He didn't mind too much. A whole world of "things" was there for him to learn.

"Say the letters you have learned so far," Elijah said, changing the subject.

Miles spouted the letters and their sounds from A to K in no time.

"You are *extremely* intelligent," Elijah said.

"Thank you," Miles said. He wanted to tell Elijah about his Mama Cee, but he thought he might cry instead.

"Us gotta get back to dat work, boy," Elijah laughed out.

Miles ignored the laugh, knowing Elijah was trying to make him forget about Nero.

"I wish I could have Nero's shirt," he said, remembering that it lay at the bottom of the whipping tree. Without waiting for Elijah to respond, Miles ran to retrieve the shirt and then ran back with it against his chest so Elijah could see the jagged edge of the torn garment.

"I'm keepin' it forever," he promised, out of breath, looking at the unmarked grave. His head throbbed a little. Then he realized that the rag he had tied around his temples must have fallen off. Swiftly, he pulled his shirt off over his head and slipped on Nero's, cramming the too-big shirttail into his loose pantaloons. To be sure, Nero's shirt was as scratchy as his was. He dug a shallow hole into the mound of the grave with his hands and stuck his rolled up shirt into the wet clay.

Elijah stepped up and watched him pat the mound in order.

"Here lies a good man," Elijah said soberly, saying good-bye for both of them. "May he rest in peace."

The noonday sun was casting short shadows when Miles watched his friend hoist his water bucket from the ground at the edge of the woods some distance away. He himself tucked his true feelings in a safe place and breathed in the refreshing odor of the fragrant pines.

All at once, Miles noticed that muted voices refused to sing the nonsense songs or cry out the felling of a tree with "One mo' down." The silent breakers kept their circle at a safe distance, looking suspicious but unsure of what to do with slaves that did not laugh and shout.

Cookie beckoned him from behind a pile of branches, not noticing that Miles now wore a different shirt. The boy began to untangle the branches too.

"Y'all done?" Cookie asked, hungry for any news about the burial. The cook's anticipating chin moved up and down.

"Yassar," Miles answered. He wished he could have told the leaning ear why his own shirt lay buried in the mound of Nero's grave, but he couldn't without giving away Nero's secret.

Cookie eyed him down with disappointment. The boy pulled a pinecone from a dead branch and stared at it briefly.

"Well," Cookie spoke again in an understanding tone, "we be goin' to fix fancy eats dis day. Breaker say so. Us leave nigh."

"I be ready," Miles said. He smiled easily now that the cook was not mad. "When I leave here, I be knowin' how to cook good as you, Cookie."

"You ain't know how to peel a turnip yet," Cookie chuckled. "When you plan on leavin' here, boy? Next year?"

"Right after the fancy eats," Miles answered, mocking himself.

"Well, let's build a few mo' piles, den us go," Cookie grinned, playing along with foolishness. The boy was good company.

For the next two hours they hacked the branches from

the logs and made piles almost as tall as Cookie's head.

Elijah came around with his bucket of water. "L," he whispered to Miles while Cookie drank noisily from the gourd. "Limbs, limbs, limbs," he stressed as Cookie dipped for another gourd of water.

Miles caught on to the letter and the sound of it just as before. He knew Elijah was clever enough to show him the shape of the letter without arousing suspicion.

"Y'all tryin' to outdo yo' own self?" Elijah joked out loud.

"Gotta do somethin'," Cookie said, resigned to the hard work. "I know breakers get richer and richer. Howsomever my gut feel lil' bit better wid workin'."

"You right," Elijah agreed, taking the gourd and following Cookie's looking around to see if the other men had done as much work.

Then Miles almost giggled when his friend pointed his forefinger up and stretched out his thumb to form the letter L behind Cookie's back.

"We goin' to the shed now." Miles began to tell him the bit of news.

"Yeah, to fix fancy," Elijah confirmed, slyly.

"Who tole you?"

"A bird on the wing."

"Who tole you?" Miles demanded, burning with curiosity.

"Dese men need water." Elijah ended the conversation abruptly and walked off with his bucket slung across his shoulder.

Cookie unlocked the smokehouse and gawked along with Miles at three cured hams, brown sugar, a jug of molasses, flour, eggs, a tin of melting butter, and coffee.

"I ain't never . . . ," Cookie said, at a loss for words. "Why you reckon . . . ?"

Miles knew why, but he didn't repeat what Elijah had said.

"Dis is good-tasting coffee," he said instead, sniffing the gauzy bag. "Best kind," he added as much like a man as possible.

"Coffee make young folks blockheaded," Cookie intoned absent-mindedly, staring from one ham to the other.

"They left skillets and tin plates and cups too—and a coffeepot." Miles tried to show Cookie, who leaned across the rough table with his eyes trained on the food.

Finally, Cookie straightened his body and barked eagerly, "Boy, you kindle dat fire. Us gonna have us a time. You hear me?"

Miles had to make a fire for the vegetable pot where Cookie boiled the hams first. Then he made two more fires because Cookie was afraid of burning the skillets of molasses bread and flour bread.

"Look to dat bread, boy," the cook fumed. "Fire got to cool down some."

Miles ran from one fire to the next, burning his hands sometimes when he tried to flip the flour bread or rake the hot coals away.

"Need water, boy," Cookie urged again and again. "Crack dem eggs."

Miles hardly noticed the sinking sun and the cool of the evening setting in. The aroma of the sweet bread and coffee was overlaid with smoke that made him cough and his eyes run.

Cookie was happily slicing the boiled ham when the men ambled out of the woods. The breakers were keeping their distance.

"Dey comin'," Miles warned Cookie, expecting to see the men break out in a run and to hear the usual robust shouts. The men kept their loping pace with an eerie silence that led them toward the shed. Cookie groaned like he was somehow responsible for the men's changed behavior.

No one rushed to pick up a tin plate or a cup from the table. Miles passed these new utensils out along with the wooden spoons.

One by one, he and Cookie heaped the food onto the plates as the men filed by, nodding at the flour bread and the molasses bread for seconds.

By the way the breakers were looking on in bewilderment, it was clear that the men spoke the loudest and said the most with their mouths closed. Miles was comforted to see that Elijah had melted into the group like it was all right to show his feelings for once.

Out of respect, Miles quietly poured coffee into cups thickly coated at the bottom with brown sugar. He fixed a plate for himself and for Cookie and poured himself a cup of coffee.

The boy joined the men at the woodpile and sat on the ground, carefully balancing his plate and his precious cup. He was taking his third swig of coffee when, suddenly, a hand reached over his shoulder and lifted the cup from his fingers.

"Coffee make you blockheaded," Cookie scolded. "Ain't ol' 'nuff for no coffee."

"I be twelve," Miles said amid a stream of chuckles from the men.

"You ain't nothin' but a lil' snapper," one of the men said. "Us gotta look out for you."

"How old I got to be 'fore I get to drinking coffee?" Miles half begged.

"Ol' like me," Elijah answered for Cookie, who poured the remaining coffee into his own cup.

Miles could do nothing but laugh. Cookie reminded him of Mrs. Bethenia. He felt contented that the men had accepted him. Somehow, it seemed like he was part of a celebration. He listened to the quiet chatter and learned some of their names like Jarvis, Prince, Edward, and all. Nero was not mentioned. Miles could sense that all had learned about Nero's secret—all except Cookie.

"Lease you know yo' age," Cookie wedged in to him, loudly. "I wisht I knowed mine."

"Didn't nobody ever tell you?" Miles asked, noticing

that the men were kindly paying attention.

Cookie mulled over the question before he answered.

"Dey said I be thirty, first time sold. Next time dey sell me I be twenty-five—long time back. Y'all see my gray hair. Dat prove I ain't twenty-five no mo'."

The men looked Cookie up and down, figuring his years of living. Miles had no one to compare Cookie to except Bounty, and not one of the men appeared as old as the slave tracker.

"I reckon you 'bout fifty-five or sixty," one of the younger men said helpfully. "Ol' slavers lie and say you young when you ain't so dey can sell you at top price. Dey say I was nineteen but my old grandma say I was twenty-six when dey put me on the block."

Suddenly, Cookie jumped up and began to scrub the table. Greasy water splashed onto the hot coals, sending whiffs of steam into the dusky air. The deep voices faded away as the men eyed more breakers than usual easing a smaller circle around them, guns drawn. There were at least ten of them.

"Whar you at, boy?" Cookie shouted desperately. "Rinse off dem plates and all."

"Yassar," Miles said, scrambling to pick up the dishes, hoping that his quick movement would stop Cookie from acting so scared.

Avery and Burgess stood wide-legged at the barn door, counting the men who were walking in as slowly as they could.

"Did you bury him deep, boy—like I told you?" Cobb asked, sneering.

"Yassar," Miles answered quickly, rinsing the cups at the well.

"I'm not talkin' to you," Cobb said in a low growl.

Astounded, the boy looked up to see Elijah standing on the other side of the well.

"He be buried deep, Mist' Cobb," his friend said, without feeling.

"What's wrong with you boys?" Cobb asked, irritated. "I just give you a good meal—better than any of you ever ate—and all y'all did was—"

"Good meal, good meal, best ever," Elijah swore with an earnest look on his face. Cobb grunted and turned away, deciding not to threaten further.

Miles felt ashamed for the men, called boys and forced to behave like boys. A few days ago, he thought he had known all there was to know about being a slave. Now it seemed that he learned a new twist every few hours. He wondered if he could ever untangle himself from all this.

Cookie tossed the last dishes in the shed and locked the door.

"Put water on dem hot coals, boy," he ordered as if the breakers could hear him. Then the cook half ran toward the barn before Miles could say, "Yassar."

Miles untied the pulley to the well. The rope slithered through his fingers and sank the bucket into the deep water.

The heavy meal did not give him enough energy to tug the full bucket but halfway. He held on to the rope and braced his feet against the well casing while he rested.

Someone cleared his throat.

"Elijah?" the boy whispered.

"Nobody but me, lil' brother," Elijah said rising up from behind the well, grinning.

"You got another letter for me," Miles stated, still hanging on to the rope.

"No letter this time," Elijah said, shedding his slave talk as he slid around to pull the bucket out of the well.

"Your brow appears to be distressed. Is your head troubling you?" he asked, concerned.

"No, my head is not troubled," Miles said, picking up the word clues and trying to copy Elijah's speech pattern. "My mind's troubled."

"What's wrong?" Elijah asked, dousing the hot coals. They headed toward the barn.

"The breakers call everybody 'boy,'" Miles blurted out. "That made me feel shame for y'all."

"Do you feel like a boy?"

"Yes, because I am a boy."

"The breakers can call you boy, slave, king, emperor, fool, or dog mess. Now then, if you don't feel like what those names imply, you are not."

"Yes, but Cobb called you 'boy' too," Miles frowned, countering Elijah.

Elijah lowered his voice to say, "Do you suppose so many breakers with guns would be needed to guard boys?" Elijah hurried on, "The breakers are afraid of men, not boys."

"But that means if I don't feel like a slave, I am not a slave?" He was sorry that it was too dark for him to see Elijah's mouth form the concise words.

"That is correct. So then, you are someone who is being held against his wishes—the same as for all of us who do not feel like slaves."

"I am not a slave," the boy stated, trying to believe his own words.

Elijah cleared his throat, letting Miles know that the conversation was over. Avery and Burgess were waiting as they entered the well-lit barn a half minute later.

# Chapter 6

Over the next two weeks, Miles learned the remaining letters of the alphabet by Elijah's cleverness. Before long he could read words that he scratched on the ground under Elijah's instructions.

Soon an intense desire to learn replaced fear as Miles' constant companion. He could string letters together to form words. Still Elijah cautioned the boy to stay alert.

It seemed that new faces joined the circle every day. When they least expected it, a breaker would pop around a tree or sneak up from behind and suddenly turn in another direction without saying a word. After a while this trickery did not frighten Miles as much, but Cookie would break out in cold sweats. The men felled about as many trees as before but without the rollicking songs.

Elijah had been right about the breakers paying for Nero's death. Late one afternoon, all of the axes fell silent when a white man arrived and called Cobb out of the woods.

"You owe me six hundred dollars," the man yelled angrily. "I sent Nero here for you to break him out his rambunctious spirit. I didn't send him here to die."

"He was a runner," Cobb responded and led the man, fussing all the way, to one of the clapboard houses.

"He wasn't here but three weeks before you killed him," the man choked out like he was grieving. By that time, they could not make out what Cobb and the white man said. The men made up their own ending to the story.

That night, Miles heard scuffling and dragging noises. He thought he must be dreaming. Then a loud thud sounded in the barn. He jackknifed up to see four tall dark figures tussling with someone in the dim light at the barn's doorway. Quickly the door closed behind them with an echoing squeak. Miles looked around. Not one of the men had stirred. Miles lay on his side and stared at the barn door. "I hope nobody don't mess wid me," he thought. Fear kept him awake.

At last, morning came. The men bustled around the stewpot with their bowls and spoons, not mentioning the night before. Miles searched the crowd for Elijah, hoping to get some answers for his questions.

"Look yonder!" Cookie suddenly blurted out, pointing and forgetting the nearby breakers. Miles followed Cookie's gaze to see the man, Jarvis, stagger out of the hay field, his eyes swollen shut.

"Get to your work," Cobb growled.

Miles and Cookie found no more cured hams in the smokehouse, though twice a jug of molasses or coffee was placed inside the shed. Then they were back to digging into the keg of dried fish and salt pork and sifting through the wormy cornmeal. The men had been allowed to bathe themselves with homemade soap and were given a change of clothing, but Miles refused to give up Nero's shirt. The breakers didn't notice.

Eight days had passed since the night Miles witnessed Jarvis being taken from the barn. Mike could not erase from his mind the sight of him staggering out of the field. Cookie was frightened, too. As Miles and Cookie prepared the evening meal, they heard the men leaving the woods, humming together like one voice in four parts. The breakers didn't like that so they shot into the air to break up the harmony. The shots scared Cookie almost into fits.

"Dey kill us all," he moaned, wrapping his arms around his head and falling onto the ground.

"No dey ain't." Miles tried to help the older man to his feet. "See, dey still livin'," he said, nodding toward the men. "Jest ain't singin', dat's all."

Cookie refused to look in the direction of the guns.

"I am not a slave," Miles said to strengthen himself against the tentacles of fear that reached out from Cookie's falling-down space. "I don't feel like a slave."

With the cook babbling to himself like a baby, Miles did most of the work. Finally, the evening meal was served and the bowls and spoons were cleaned.

"Cookie done gone fool," Miles heard one of the men say what everybody knew already.

That night, the cook so disturbed the barn with his

moaning and groaning the men could not sleep. When Cobb stood over the pile of hay to threaten him, Cookie jumped about screaming, "Please, massa, don't y'all shoot me!"

"Leave him be!" one voice rang out, then another, and another until the barn vibrated with the chant, drowning out Cookie's screams.

Cobb backed off.

The next day, in the late afternoon, six weeks after Cookie had arrived at the breaking ground, a breaker led him out of the woods. And the cook returned to the plantation, wherever it was, a "broken" man.

Miles wondered about the sort of man Cookie was before he was sent to the breaking ground and if the cook had a real name. He went back to hacking at the branches and reminding himself, "I don't feel like a slave," when Elijah cut into his thoughts.

"You reckon you and me can fix eats dis day, boy?" Elijah dangled the key to the shed.

"You the cook," Miles confirmed, hiding his gladness. "Who gonna give us water?" All he could think about was the opportunity to learn from his friend every day. Now, more than ever.

"One dey call Prince gonna be water boy," Elijah answered, picking up Cookie's axe and glancing here and there.

Miles knew that someone was in earshot by Elijah's dancing eyes and slave talk. The boy sank his axe into a meaty limb.

"Elijah?" Avery called from nearby.

"Yassar!" Elijah answered on the swing of his axe.

"You be sure to pile up as many limbs as Cookie or more, you understand me?"

"Yassar!"

"I got my eyes on you, and my gun," Avery said coolly, slapping the gun.

Miles flinched a little.

"Yassar!" Elijah shouted, putting an edge of fear in his tone.

Avery said no more. Chopping axes echoed from one end of the now skimpy woods to the other. The sun was boring large holes of glaring light between the fallen trees when they left their axes in the woods.

Aside from unlocking the smokehouse door, Miles found out that Elijah didn't know the first thing about preparing food for people to eat. Yet he was determined to handle the entire meal by himself. He told Miles to kindle the fire under the hanging pot and to tote the water from the well.

The boy smiled to himself when his friend boldly pared a few of the large, oval turnips down to little balls. Cookie would have gone into a conniption at such waste.

"Peeling too much away, Elijah," Miles cautioned, inspecting the thick peelings.

"Suggestion taken," Elijah said, confidently withdrawing the sharp blade a bit.

After so many suggestions like "put in the meat first . . . too much water . . . stir from the bottom of the pot . . .

dumplings go in the pot last . . . pot scorching," Miles asked, "Breakers know you can't cook?"

"Of course not," Elijah laughed. "I told Cobb I was the best cook on this side of the Wettown River. Besides, you have taught me how to prepare these measly morsels." Elijah mocked the bubbly stew with a grand hand gesture.

The sound of woodcutters echoed across the hay field. Soon they would have to serve the hungry men.

"Let's eat," Miles urged his friend. "Then you can show me how to make words with the letters I know."

"I do not expect to depart from these illustrious breaking grounds until you have learned to read and write," Elijah said, continuing his mockery of their plight.

"But you might leave soon," Miles said, dipping two bowls of stew. He pushed a pitiful image of Cookie out of his memory, but his stomach began to quiver like it had a mind of its own no matter how hard he tightened his muscles. He handed a brimming bowl of stew and a wooden spoon to Elijah.

"What's this we are eating?" Elijah asked, frowning as he scooped some of the food to his lips.

"Stew," Miles said eagerly, knowing a lesson had begun by the tone of Elijah's voice.

"Listen to the sound of the word. St-ew. What letters do you hear?"

"S-T-U," Miles said, tasting the hot meal.

Elijah scratched the correct spelling in the dirt. "If this

word is st-ew, what is this word?" he asked, scratching another word into the dirt.

"Few!" Miles shouted, almost tipping his bowl over.

"You done cookin', boy?" Cobb threatened from the dog pen.

"Yassar," Elijah said, standing up to watch Cobb approach them. "It be ready, Mist' Cobb," Elijah assured, dropping his head and wiping his feet on the words. "All dey got to do is eat."

"Well, since you finished so quick, you can leave the woods later tomorrow," Cobb said, turning away to take his position.

"Then it'll be too dark to see the words," Miles whispered, even though Cobb was some distance away.

"You didn't hear what he said." Elijah accused Miles. "He said later. Later is an indefinite term. He didn't say how much later."

Soon bowls were shoved at the pot so fast Miles and Elijah were spattered with the hot stew more than once. After eating, the men tossed the bowls and spoons aside and walked to the barn not talking.

The chilly wind searched the inside of Miles' shirt, making it puff out like he was on a clothesline. It was dark now.

"Miles," Elijah said, turning the key in the lock of the shed door. "I am helping you to learn, but you must watch out for yourself when you're with me and when you are not with me."

"You scared?" Miles asked, believing his friend would tell him the truth.

"Show me a man who does not consider fear to be worthy and I'll show you a fool," Elijah answered.

Miles asked again, "You scared? Yes or no."

"No," Elijah said. "I can't say 'yes or no.' However, we shall discuss the issue of fear one day soon. Right now, little brother, think about all you are going to learn."

That night, Miles lay on his pile of hay, thinking, "Elijah never give a straight-out answer, just like Macon." During training Macon used to answer yes or no questions with "maybe, maybe not." It occurred to Miles that he had not thought about the great house and the servants-in-training for a long while. Not a day passed that he did not think about Mama Cee. He had never told anyone at the breaking ground about her—not even Elijah.

The boy stared at the ceiling, picturing the way Elijah had scratched the words STEW and FEW into the dirt. The word DEW dropped into his mind by itself. Then, RAT and CAT, FAT, HAT followed to his amazement. He closed his eyes to stop the words from falling into his imagination. He could hardly catch his breath. In spite of tightening his eyelids, MOP and HOP squeezed in. The words were so clear he could almost reach out and touch them now. Words beginning with every letter of the alphabet danced around his pile-of-hay bed. The boy bolted upright and looked around in the dim lantern light, not able to control his racing mind. He almost felt like someone could hear his thoughts.

"I got to tell Elijah," Miles said out loud as if in a stupor.

"You losing your senses too, boy?" Cobb growled at him, thinking Miles was talking in his sleep.

"Yas-yassar," Miles stuttered, falling on his back, not knowing how long the breaker had been watching. He surely did not wish to be questioned further.

Before daylight the next morning, Miles was wide-awake when Elijah nudged him. The boy whispered his discovery of sound-alike words all the way to the shed. All the while he drew the spelling of the words in the air.

"You are ready to learn larger words," Elijah praised.

"I can read some," the boy whispered excitedly.

"You are preparing to read," Elijah said.

Without warning, the weather had changed from sunny to bone-chilling cold—especially during early morning and late afternoon. The breakers left a heap of old, moldy pantaloons and shirts at the barn door for them to pick over. To keep warm, they all decked themselves out in more than two outfits.

"Us look lika bunch o' fat, black crows," Prince laughed out when he came around with the water.

Grimly Miles spelled out, "P-R-I-N-S C-R-O-W" as soon as the new "water boy" lugged his bucket away.

"P-R-I-N-C-E," Elijah corrected in a low voice without smiling. "And Prince is making the best of a bad situation.

Laughter makes a light heart."

Instantly guilt lined the boy's face. Then he became righteous again with, "Well, I am not black like a crow—I'm brown."

"You are just as black as Cobb is white," Elijah said. "You've never heard him deny that fact, have you?"

Miles could not pluck an answer from his mind right then, but he suspected that Elijah would lead him into feelings he did not want to face. Now that he thought about it, all of the servants and the servants-in-training had skin the same color as his or lighter. Not one of them was as dark as Prince was.

"Come 'ere, boy," Avery called.

Miles looked up from his deep thoughts. Avery was standing between two trees, looking at him. "Got to watch out for myself," he thought, dropping an armload of prickly branches. He trudged within a few feet of Avery.

"Is that fish keg empty, boy?"

"Yassar." Miles remembered that they had thrown the last of the dried fish into the pot that morning.

"Well, you go up there and set the keg out," Avery ordered.

"Yassar," Miles said, avoiding Avery's eyes. He clutched the shed key Elijah tossed to him.

"Put some spunk in you, you lil' devil. I'm looking for you back 'fore you get there."

Miles broke into a trot. For some unknown reason the key

lodged in the door lock and wouldn't turn one way or the other. Beads of sweat popped out on his brow. Going back to tell Avery about the jammed lock would be dangerous. He attempted to twist the key a few more times. At last, the lock cracked opened. Miles pulled on the door and stumbled to the far side of the shed to the fishy-smelling keg.

"That's what I told John Cobb to do," a bragging laugh squeezed out, just outside the shed. Footsteps moved to the rear.

Miles crouched behind the keg. "Breakers," he figured to himself. The door was ajar. He could tell by the easy chatter that they didn't know he was in the shed.

"Make impudent darkies think they masters gonna sell 'em off, they get so scared you won't have no more trouble," another breaker said. Sounded like Burgess.

"You oughta seen 'em," the first one exclaimed and mimicked, "Yassar, Mist' Cobb, us can sing." The three of them slapped their thighs.

"What 'bout that Elijah?" a new voice asked. "Something 'bout him I don't like. I think he's slick as soap."

"He works all right but I get a funny feeling too... when I see him moving 'round so quiet like," said another voice Miles did not recognize.

"We breakin' him down like the rest of 'em. He's scared of his own footprints, jumpin' when I look at him," Burgess said, annoyed that one of his hired helpers was attempting to criticize the breaking system.

"One thing for certain," the first man said, "we gonna have plenty of timber to sell. Cobb's talkin' to the buyers in about three weeks he say. Mayhap I can buy my own self a passel of darkies."

The other breakers grunted in disbelief. Footsteps trailed off in two directions.

Miles sat still for a little while, listening to his thumping heart. Then he stole to the door and peeped out. One breaker was disappearing around the barn. He looked around the corner of the shed. Burgess and the other breakers were entering the woods. By the time he rolled the keg to the outside and locked the door, rivulets of sweat ran down his face. He tore across the field, trying to make up for lost time.

"I hope you're all right," Elijah said, snatching the key from the gasping boy.

A cracking whip spat into the air.

"Took your own sweet time, did you?" Avery demanded, walking toward them.

Elijah dropped to his knees behind a pile of limbs to pick at the small branches.

"You disobeyed me, boy." The whip cracked again. "I'ma show you how to obey me, boy," Avery snarled.

"Make noise," Elijah pushed from his hidden place. "Say something."

"Key got stuck . . . stuck bad, Mist' Avery," Miles babbled. "Lock was stuck . . . dat's what t'was. Yassar, dat's what t'was!"

Avery kept coming. The whip cracked again, nearer that time.

"Scream—faint," Elijah prodded.

*"I couldn't git de do' open!"* Miles hollered a mournful cry at the top of his lungs.

Before Avery's alarmed eyes, the boy's body sagged slowly to the ground.

"Sumthin' wrong wid de boy!" Elijah sprang up, screaming. "Mist' Cobb, Mist' Burgess, what y'all want me ta do?"

Elijah pretended not to see the "another one to pay for" look on Avery's face. Cobb and Burgess were bursting through the underbrush, ordering the men, "Get your eyes back to your work, hear me! Get back!"

"What happened to him?" Cobb panted out to no one in particular. He scanned Miles' limp body for signs of life.

"Uh, he was—" Elijah started to speak.

"Well, he ran back from the shed," Avery cut in. "I sent him to take that empty fish keg out. Maybe he got overcome from that. Some of 'em can't stand nothin'." Avery thought better of mentioning the cracking whip to Cobb.

Miles jumped and sat up when Cobb's fingers pressed the side of his sweaty throat. Elijah's sly wink told him he had "fainted" himself out of a lashing and that he was safe.

"Gotta git my axe," he heard himself say.

"Here yo' axe," Elijah chided, pressing the handle against Miles' palm. "Now git up from dere! I ain't goh do my work an' yourn too!"

85

Cobb watched the boy cut into a few branches with Elijah sprinkling, "Let dat axe go—dat's right," on him. Cobb and Avery exchanged looks and went back to the singing and falling trees.

Miles and Elijah worked under Avery's distant but hateful stare until Cobb sent them to prepare the meal. Elijah kept his silence all the way to the shed.

"I got news," Miles announced, poking in the keg of dried fish someone had filled up.

"Tell me," Elijah said tiredly.

At the end of his rush to tell all he had heard, his friend turned his face to the west.

"What you think, Elijah?"

"You say Cobb is to sell timber in about three weeks. Well, I think you and I should leave the breaking ground for a little while," Elijah said with a smile on his face.

"You know how to do that?"

"I do."

"I can't go with you, Elijah . . . see, I have to go back to Mama . . ." Miles stopped himself.

"I'm not asking you to run, Miles. You'll see."

Interested now, Miles lit into him with a hail of questions. Elijah explained simply. "Too dangerous. If I give you that information, the breakers might talk it out of you if something goes wrong. They might even make use of the lash. However, if you truly don't know, then all you can say is 'I don't know' if they were to take it upon themselves to question you."

"Never would I tell," Miles vowed, feeling hurt but relieved at the same time that he was not asked to risk never seeing Mama Cee again. He would do whatever the breakers asked—he would even sing the disgusting songs and bare his teeth into the widest grin to see Mama Cee. Now he understood why the men were acting like slaves.

# Chapter 7

That the breakers had gone back to snuffing most of the lanterns did not help Miles get to sleep that night. He lay there inventing scenes of himself and Elijah walking away to freedom with their heads held high—a book in either hand. Mama Cee was so proud of him. "You such a smart young man," he could hear her say. She held him at arm's length like he was a man, able to take care of her.

After a while, the boy lost count of the number of words and spelling rules he had learned. Elijah taught him the days of the week and the months of the year and he could count as high as he wanted to. He learned to tell precious time by studying clock faces that Elijah etched in the dirt. Often it took a day or two to read a whole sentence because Elijah could risk writing only two or three words at a time.

With Elijah's help, Miles sifted through his surroundings to put new meanings to the words he had learned to read and spell. Mansions like Gency Tillery's great house had been designed by an architect. Dogs were canines; cats, felines; rats became rodents; and an axe and a shovel were implements. The boy thought that anything as bothersome as a common housefly did not deserve to be called an insect.

Yet he could not think of a name that he would rather call a fly except, perhaps, a maggot.

Miles took to sleeping with his arm wrapped around his head to protect his knowledge.

Several weeks later, Prince was the one who nudged him to his senses with, "Gittup, boy, us gotta git up dere ta dat shed."

A minute passed before Miles could focus well enough to say, "You ain't Elijah." Besides, when the boy looked at the door, he couldn't see the crack of daylight he had been used to seeing. He turned over to go back to sleep.

Two powerful hands yanked him to his feet and thrust him into the cold air.

"I be cookin', now," Prince said like he was in charge of the whole breaking ground. He looked back to see if the sleepy boy was following.

"Where Elijah at?" Miles asked Prince, feeling confused and mad.

A well-practiced reply was thrown over the shoulder. "I spend six months o' year tendin' my own biziness and six months leavin' other folk'ses biziness 'lone."

If it had not been for the light from the fire Miles kindled, Prince would not have been able to see how to burn up the first pot of food. After scraping the crusty bottom of the pot, Miles kept muttering to himself, "Breakers ain't gonna lash me for wasting good rations." Then Prince begrudgingly stepped aside and let the boy take over.

"Miles, Miles!" Elijah suddenly called to him from the barn. "Come on heah!"

"What ail him, boy?" Prince cried fearfully, stirring from the bottom of the pot like Miles told him and glancing around for the breakers.

"I gotta go," Miles said. He didn't know why he felt a twinge of pity for Prince as he ran toward the barn, but he did. By the time he got halfway there, an onslaught of men drove him off the path. At least Prince would have company and the food was hot.

"Git in here," Elijah said in an angry tone, from inside the barn. Two breakers were standing near the door. Miles understood and entered the dimly lit barn. Instantly, he knew that he was not to mention the dark green trousers and the yellow shirt with a string bow tie his friend was wearing. He also saw a blue jacket draped across a pile of hay.

"Quick!" Elijah said loudly, handing Miles a pan of cold water with a floating bar of homemade soap. "Wash yo'self."

At a feverish pace, Miles managed to wash and dry himself with a rag.

"Put dese duds on," Elijah ordered and tossed a bundle of clothes at him.

The soft wool trousers and light-colored cotton shirt with little wooden buttons reminded him of his great house days. "What did Elijah do?" the boy asked his mind.

"Don't wear *that* shirt," Elijah whispered through his teeth.

"It won't show," Miles said, pulling the clean shirt over Nero's soiled one.

Elijah eyed the boy's lumpy shoulders.

"Take it off," he said.

"I promised to wear it forever," Miles countered, hoping that Elijah wouldn't say anymore. He ran his hand across his damp forehead, forced his arms into the jacket, and began to fasten the shirt's buttons. Elijah clicked his teeth and turned toward the barn door.

"Get up there, boys," Cobb directed them, as much like a gentleman as he could muster. He sat on the back seat of an ancient-looking, open carriage drawn by two old horses. Cobb wore an ill-fitting, dusty black great cloak and a shiny top hat. Elijah climbed into the driver's seat and grabbed the reins.

"Drive on," Cobb ordered, keeping his gentleman's tone.

Miles wished he could see Cobb's face from where he sat on the carriage seat with Elijah.

Elijah clicked his tongue. The horses pulled off, one walking two paces ahead of the other. Elijah tried to even out the animals by slackening the left rein and holding the other taut. It was a cloudy morning. Soon the familiar foulness of the Wettown River blew onto dry land. After a while, they could see the murky water lapping against the soft banks. Big white birds flapped their wings in the distant sky. Miles searched the water for a barge that looked like the one Elijah had drawn in the dirt and saw none. The boy began to burn with curiosity. He surely couldn't read Cobb's face. Elijah's smooth brown face didn't tell him anything either.

The horses held to a mismatched gait.

"Keep to the right," Cobb ordered when the road forked.

Looking ahead of the horses, Miles could see that the road was about to change to red bricks. He was going to Wettown. "Mayhap Cobb be sellin' his lumber in town," he thought. His eyes followed the brick patterns into town.

Suddenly Cobb ordered, "Turn into the livery stable."

Miles coughed and bit his tongue to keep from reading aloud the large sign that said, "COBURN'S LIVERY." Tears blurred the smaller print, but he could make out, "Fine oats served here. 25 Cents Per Day." He could read, even if the words were not written in the dirt. His body twisted around so as to catch sight of other signs.

"Pay 'tention!" his friend said, jabbing him in the ribs.

Cobb's derisive grunt approved.

Miles could not understand why the tears would not stop rolling down his face. He was not in pain. He was not scared or angry. He didn't feel hungry though the sun was almost two hours high. To be sure, old folks cried for happiness, not him.

He gave way to embarrassment when Elijah had to nudge him two times to open the carriage door for Cobb. Even so, the tears continued to flow as Cobb stepped down, tipping the carriage to one side with his weight.

"What ails him now?" the breaker asked.

"Somethin' got in his eyes back dere, Mist' Cobb," Elijah said quickly. "He be all right. He hard workin'."

"Any day now," Cobb said hatefully to Miles, ignoring Elijah, "Mister Tillery's gonna send somebody to take you out of my sight. Why your master sent somebody as young and simple as you, I do not know. I almost want to give him his money back. You ain't had no spirit when you come to my place and you won't have none when you go back."

At hearing he was going to see his Mama Cee, Miles almost sobbed.

"Yassar, Mist' Cobb!" he gushed, wiping his eyes for the last time. "My eye some better! Yassar! Here go yo' bag, Mist' Cobb."

Cobb snatched the small valise from Miles' fingers and handed it up to Elijah.

"Stable the horses, Elijah," he ordered. "Then bring the bag to me at the depot office as planned."

"We got to pay money, Mist' Cobb?" Elijah asked meekly.

Cobb dug two fingers into his vest pocket.

"Whatever Elijah doin', us gonna git caught," Miles thought.

"Pay Mister Coburn two bits," Cobb instructed. "And use

two bits to buy you and this trembling fool something to eat. I'll tell you where when you find me at the depot."

Miles looked back at the big man as he crossed the empty brick street lined with shops. He saw Cobb walk between two tall buildings as the horses pulled the carriage into the livery stable.

"Elijah, I'm going back to the plantation," Miles said as they were leaving the stable. "And I can read words no matter where they are."

"I know," Elijah said. "I saw you reading."

Miles tried to explain, "I was crying because—"

"Miles," Elijah stopped him, "any man, woman, or child born without tears would be in pretty bad shape. Tears are not necessarily a sign of weakness. Tears can show strength too. How you feel about your tears is your business."

Miles, as usual, was at a loss for words when Elijah directed him to make up his own mind. But for once he felt that he *could* figure his feelings out. He just couldn't talk about them right then.

"You saw where he went," Elijah said, swinging the valise. "Lead on, little man."

"Don't know if I can." Miles walked ahead. "I ain't got no spirit, you know."

"If you had mor'n you already got, they'd put you in the lockup," Elijah laughed as they followed Cobb's path to the depot.

"Now listen," Elijah said seriously. "I can tell you as much

94

as you have suspected. I convinced Cobb that he needed us to show how important he is when he meets these lumber buyers."

"How did you convince him?" Miles wondered out loud, awed by Elijah's bravery. "He is the meanest man I ever seen."

"Never mind the meanness," his friend said quietly. "You and I are in Wettown today, dressed in these better-looking duds. We will do his fetchin' and totin'."

"Elijah, I want to be free," Miles blurted out, wanting to show his own bravery.

"Not now," Elijah said between his teeth, lifting his shoulders as they mounted the platform. Miles recognized the railroad tracks. Elijah faced three outside doors. He did the same.

"What you darkies want?" a cigar-smoking white man asked, emerging from behind the end door.

"Lookin' for Mist' Cobb," Elijah said, staring the man in the eye.

"Which Mister Cobb? Two or three of them 'round here."

"Mister John Cobb," Miles spoke up, enjoying Elijah's raised eyebrows.

The man pointed to the middle door and watched Elijah knock gently.

As soon as the door opened Elijah led him toward Cobb, who was chatting with a group of men dressed in dark outfits. Rings of cigar smoke spread through the small room furnished with stuffed, high-backed chairs and two oaken desks.

"Hey! What you doing, boy?" the indignant door opener called after them. The room grew quiet and eyes pointed to Elijah.

"I be 'liverin' dis bag to Mist' John Cobb," Elijah turned and announced to the irritated man. "He powerful busy. I be 'proachin' him if you don' mind." With that, Elijah turned away from the insulted door opener and marched to Cobb. Miles figured out that no one was about to mess with Elijah in front of Cobb.

"Dey tell us ta git here quick as us could, Mist' Cobb," Elijah said in a low tone.

Cobb stepped a few feet away from the group. Miles could see that the men were trying to make out what Elijah was saying. They stared at the papers Cobb pulled out of the bag.

"These are the offers to buy lumber I need right now," Cobb said, studying and shifting the papers. "Follow me— you hear me," Cobb said and walked toward the door with Elijah and Miles behind him.

"Mister Cobb, are you departing?" one member of the group called out, speaking in clipped words. The boy couldn't take the chance of giving the man a second look.

"Give me a few minutes, gentlemen," Cobb said politely while he scribbled on one of the papers with a stubby pencil. Elijah opened the door and the three of them headed for the steps that led away from the tracks.

All the while, Miles had been trying to figure out for himself what was to happen next. Everything was so confusing and exciting. Elijah was as slick as soap, just like the breakers said.

"Put this in your pocket, boy," Cobb said, stealing a look at the man on the platform.

"I need ta know what writ on it?" Elijah whispered cautiously.

"Naw," Cobb answered. "Got to keep them guessing," he whispered. "You go 'round yonder." He pointed to some buildings. "Wait at the back door and somebody will hand you something to eat. When you hear that train coming, get back here to me—quick."

Miles walked ahead, thinking about the train he might catch sight of. He and Elijah sat on the wobbly stairs and waited. Elijah leaned back on his elbows and closed his eyes. Food smells floated down to them.

Impatiently, Miles jumped off the steps to examine an old, broken cart wheel that sprawled in the small, trashy yard. He kicked and scattered a clump of decaying burlap sacks. Under the sacks were damp, mangled sheets of paper from what appeared to be a book of some sort. It was not leather-bound but softbacked and not as thick as he remembered the books to be at the great house library. "*Harper's New Monthly Magazine,* June 1850" was written across the front.

The image of Gency Tillery pulling on the bell cord drove him back to the steps in a hurry.

"Go up dere and knock on dat do'," Elijah said, watching shadows move across steamed-up windowpanes overhead. "Mayhap dey don't know us be out here."

"I saw something . . . over there," Miles said, standing before his friend, not pointing and forgetting to speak in slave dialect. "A book, I think." He stuck on the last words carefully.

Elijah stood up, gazing at the trash pile.

"I am going to pick it up," Miles said before Elijah could move another inch to stop him.

The boy sealed the cold book between his skin and Nero's shirt as the door opened outward.

"Here 'tis!" a cheerful cry rang out. They looked up to see a dark-skinned, buxom woman with a gap in her front teeth. She extended two napkin-wrapped clay bowls. Miles ran to climb the steps, two at a time.

"Thanky, ma'am." He nodded, taking the bowls.

"I can't let y'all in here—Mist' Cobb know dat too," she said with an apology in her tone. "Y'all git done, knock, an' I come take dese bowls."

"You got coffee?" Elijah asked, tossing up the two bits that Cobb had given him.

She threw up a hand to catch the money and laughed out, "Hold still!" like she had forgotten something.

"Two cups—plenty sugar and cream!" Miles yelled at the closing door.

The coffee was strong and sweet. Each swallow pumped new life into him. "Gotta git free," Miles breathed to himself. Instantly, he noticed happily that he had trained himself to think in field-hand dialect. Maybe he would need that kind of protection for the rest of his life—something to hide behind.

"Eats git cold," Elijah reminded him.

"Awright," Miles said. He had kept his vow to learn how to read. By wanting a share in learning he had made it come to him, with Elijah's help. But now he had to find a way to tell his own feet where to go. "Can't go free, lessen Mama Cee wid me," he said to himself.

He resisted the temptation to pat the left side of his torso where the book rested against his rib cage. He wondered when he would be able to fold back the thin pages and just look at the words. In his mind, Mama Cee's face was shining as she watched him read.

"What you grinnin' 'bout?" Elijah asked.

"Somethin'," Miles said, yet he could not mention Mama Cee.

"You be leavin' ol' Cobb and dem 'fore long," Elijah tried to catch the boy's smile.

"Leavin' you too, Elijah," Miles said slowly, freeing his mind to realize that Elijah would not be at his side much longer. How could he get along without his friend and teacher?

"You know what ol' folks say," Elijah said. "Every good-bye ain't gone."

"What you mean?" Miles asked, liking the beat of the words.

"It means that you will hear from me from time to time once you return to the Tillery Plantation," Elijah said, looking around. "Don't ask questions. I know you want freedom and I believe I can help you to find your way to freedom in the north," Elijah said.

A faraway whistle sounded. Miles ran to knock on the door. He placed the dishes on the top stair and joined Elijah at the bottom of the steps.

Wettown was stirring when they rounded the corner and headed for the station.

Cobb spent most of that day surrounded by groups of men while Elijah and Miles served as his messengers under a cold, drizzling sky. Like Elijah told him, Miles said, "Dis paper from Mist' Cobb," no matter how many times he had to hand a scrolled paper to the cigar-smoking men. Some of the men swore after glancing at the paper, but Miles did not change his calm expression.

He had taken the first step to where he wanted to go. To him, freedom was somewhere beyond the Tillery Plantation. Elijah said freedom was in the north. That's where he wanted to go.

The journey back to the breaking ground was layered in lightheartedness. Evidently, things had gone well for Cobb. He was singing-happy and celebrating by swigging from a flask of whiskey. Elijah had succeeded in gaining Cobb's trust. Miles had found a book. Only Cobb could talk about his happiness.

"Elijah, you the smartest darkie I ever seen, without no book learning too," Cobb praised jovially. "You can't read no book, but you shore can read people. If your master 'gree, I aim to buy you. You'd be my first darkie."

"Mayhap so, Mist' Cobb," Elijah sang out, just as happy. "Mayhap so."

Miles wondered the questions he knew that his friend would never answer. Who is Elijah's master? How did Elijah know all he knew without his master knowing about it?

Two days later, during the morning meal, Miles saw Bounty perched on the seat of the buckboard at the barn. The boy felt like shouting to the old man and to the mule too. A breaker was nearby.

"Don't forgit what I done told you," Elijah instructed, moving with him toward the barn. Miles glanced back at the men that stood around the fire, pretending not to notice that he, at least, wanted to say good-bye to them.

"Howdy, Miles," Bounty said, for the sake of manners.

"Howdy, Mist' Bounty," Miles replied, climbing aboard the wagon. Miles and Elijah did not say another word to each other.

Miles was quiet until the Long-Ways Road had taken them to the other side of Wettown. The sun was about three hours high when Miles asked, finally, "Mama Cee awright?"

"She be fine," Bounty said dryly. "De great house dere fa ye."

Miles swallowed hard and ground his back teeth. Elijah had told him to become a field hand—the most hated position on any plantation.

"Why?" he had asked, looking forward to a soft bed and good meals.

"I can't get to you if you're forever under the scrutiny of house servants," Elijah had warned. "A field hand has a wider range of movement. Trust no one, but make friends. Have yourself dismissed from Gency Tillery's house as soon as the opportunity arises. You know what I mean."

Miles knew exactly what Elijah meant. After all, he had learned to hide his true feelings so well that even the breakers thought he was of no account. The slave men thought the same.

How Elijah was going to make contact with him, he did not know. This fact did not worry him. The longing for freedom shaped his faith.

Instinctively, he shifted his torso so as to sense the weight of the *Harper's New Monthly Magazine.* It was not there. After rereading the few pages many times, he knew that he could not keep the magazine without risking his life. He had decided to lay it on the fire at the shed the day before. Elijah had watched the flames turn blue.

"I see you're burning knowledge," his friend said offhandedly.

"Not burning up my head," Miles had said, trying to agree with his own decision. "That's where the knowledge is."

He saved his favorite line from the magazine to think about from time to time: "This magazine is for those with intellectual curiosity and concern for issues and ideas."

# Chapter 8

A few field hands were carrying wood into their cabins in the dusk when Miles rapped lightly on Mama Cee's cabin door, waited, and rapped again. They paid him no attention, but he knew that within a few minutes everybody in the quarters would know that he had returned. The sound of barking dogs came from the other side of the great house.

"Who's there?" his Mama Cee answered at last.

"Me—Miles."

And there she was, his Mama Cee with her arms outstretched, crying in jubilation. He allowed himself to be half dragged into the candlelit cabin while she hugged, kissed, and slapped his face. He could not utter one word. His vision blurred.

"What you cryin' about? I knew you'd come back," she said at last, standing back to get a full view of him. "You growed taller and thickened up too."

He felt his face, thinking the wetness had come from her tears of happiness.

"I had to work so hard," he said, wiping his eyes and wishing he could see a reflection of himself.

"You go to the great house tonight?"

"Bounty said for me to come here."

Mama Cee spread one of her freshly made corn shuck mattresses on the floor and blew out the candle. They talked for a while. He could not attach faces to the three field hands that had run away soon after he left for the breaking ground, but he felt glad for the two men and a woman she named. Bounty had given her the message. She was surprised someone like Bounty could do "such a nice thing."

Abruptly, he heard her deep, even breathing and knew she had fallen asleep.

He dozed fitfully all night long. No amount of twisting and turning could make his body familiar with the new mattress that was so much better than his pile of hay.

Just before daybreak, he awoke to see Mama Cee slipping out of the door.

"I'm goin' with you, Mama Cee," he said, jumping up and wedging his feet into his shoes that were now getting too small.

"No, don't," Mama Cee warned.

"I can help you 'til they tell me what else to do," he said, walking beside her.

"You cold?" she asked, pressing her hand on the back of his three rough shirts.

"I ain't cold, Miss Lady," he said jokingly, patting the castoff cloak that he had been seeing her wear for years.

"Well, Jack Frost finished killin' everything that had to do with green 'round here," she said.

"Yes, ma'am," he said.

"You not nervous no more," she said suddenly.

"No, ma'am."

"You got a crackle in your voice too," she said. "I heard it first off, last night. Your manhood days not far from now."

"I know," Miles said uncomfortably. He wondered if she had seen the Adam's apple jutting out from his neck.

"I'm satisfied," she said.

"About what?"

"Maybe they learned you somethin' at that breakin' ground, but they didn't break you."

They neared the large cauldrons. Miles was glad that she could not see his face.

He was pulling the third bucket of water out of the well when Bounty coughed out, "I be comin' ta fetch ye, boy. Dey 'pectin' ye nigh."

Macon was the first to speak while the servants-in-training gaped at his ill-fitting, soiled clothing. Napoleon and Jake smirked.

"So here you are, ready to mind your manners and the rules I hope," Macon said with authority.

"Mornin' to y'all," Miles grinned, sweeping his hand and reminding them of their poor manners.

"His hands look like he's been walking on them and he talk like a field hand," a new girl blurted out before she burst into giggles.

Mrs. Bethenia quieted the girl with a piercing look.

"As soon as Miles takes a bath and dresses himself in decent clothes, he will begin to learn again how not to talk like a field hand in Gency Tillery's great house," she said curtly.

Amused, Miles waited for Mrs. Bethenia to finish placing her words like the lady in waiting Elijah had told him about. He had not intended to speak like a field hand. It just slipped out naturally.

"Mayhap dey send me way from here if my talkin' ain't pleasin' dem," he thought. The idea floated around in his head.

Soon he was sitting in a wooden tub of warm, sudsy water.

"Wash your head too," Macon stuck his head around the bathing room door to say.

"Yassar, Mist' Macon," he answered in a humble tone.

Macon's head bounced around the door for a second look at the boy.

"What *is* wrong with him?" Miles heard the trainer say as his footsteps headed for the kitchen.

Miles dried himself and slipped on the soft wool trousers and sparkling white shirt that had been lying lengthwise on his bed, not forgetting Nero's shirt first. The great house shoes were too tight for his wide feet, but he forced them to fit again without too much discomfort.

Macon, Mrs. Bethenia, and the servants-in-training were waiting for him. He sat down to the eyes staring at his bulging white shirt. No one said a word to him while the hot breakfast dishes were being passed.

He ate heartily, using the spoon and fork.

Mrs. Bethenia turned out to be the most patient woman in the world. She accompanied him everywhere during his chores. No matter how many times he feigned the mistake of saying, "I is . . . here I be . . . where tat? . . . yassar," she was at his side, encouraging him to speak correctly. Many times she praised him even after he erred. Toward the end of the day, Miles was so worn out by her patience he decided to "learn how to speak like a servant-in-training at Gency Tillery's great house."

Gency Tillery and Ol' Miss did not show themselves that day. He was not surprised. Sometimes days passed before servants-in-training would catch sight of them.

Miles was assigned to the drawing room the next day. While polishing the last paneled wall next to the door, he overheard Macon telling Mrs. Bethenia about a meeting.

"Biggest men 'round Tillery meeting here, tomorrow." Macon let the news leak out of the side of his mouth.

"I wonder for what," Mrs. Bethenia thought out loud.

"Masters in a bind about runaways and talk of uprisings," Macon said with a tinge of sympathy for the masters.

"We don't have to worry about the servants here," Mrs. Bethenia bragged softly.

"Even so, you come to me with anything you hear or see that don't look right," Macon said sternly. "I'll tell the master." The sound of two pairs of feet clicked out of Miles' earshot.

"They feel like slaves," he thought, creeping out of the drawing room and up the attic steps to the row of beds. Since he was considered to be new, Macon had to inspect his work and tell him what to do next. Miles paced the attic floor with an ear trained on the stairs.

"I don't care about the good eats and the soft bed and the fine duds," he whispered to himself. He had to find a way to be dismissed without arousing suspicion. Nero's rough shirt made his skin tingle, making him scratch his back.

Suddenly, he felt like he was being watched and whirled around. There stood Macon with an unreadable expression on his face.

"I am done with the drawing room, Macon," Miles said respectfully.

"I inspected," Macon approved.

"Well?" Miles asked, waiting to be given another chore.

"Well, I want to know what's wrong with your shirt." Macon spoke like a cat who had caught a mouse. "Take it off."

With nimble fingers, Miles unbuttoned the shirt, leaving Nero's shirt exposed.

"Tell me why you are wearing a raggedy, smelly shirt under your *clean, white* shirt," Macon demanded. "You got lice on you?"

"It reminds me," Miles said simply.

"Reminds you of what?"

"Wrongdoing." The boy dragged out the conversation, thinking as fast as he could.

When Macon responded with eyes that could melt iron, Miles jumped into his just-made-up story.

"You see, I was sent to the breaking ground because I opened a book. That was wrong. Every time this shirt scratches me, I remember that I can't break the rules. That's why I wear it."

Macon pursed his lips and looked away before he said, "Tonight, I want you to wash that stinking shirt with the sweetest soap we got up here. I'll see that it dries near the fire. You been broken. Now get yourself back together— you hear me?"

"Yes, sir," Miles said.

That was the closest any of them had come to asking how he had fared at the breaking ground. As he helped polish the silverware, Miles realized that hiding his angry feelings was not an easy thing to do at the great house. To get what was rightfully his, he had to behave like a fool every step of the way. Slow-boiling dissatisfaction knotted the muscles in his arms.

"Hey, Miles, you bending the spoons," Jake accused.

"Go tell Macon," Napoleon advised, slyly.

Without a word, Miles retrieved two bent silver spoons from the velvety rack and straightened the delicate handles with his bare hands. He put them back with the other spoons.

"Those spoons still don't look right," Napoleon continued, hoping to see Macon enter the room.

"Pick out the ones that don't look right," Miles challenged his former friend. He was not about to waste any more words on the likes of Napoleon and Jacob or any of them at the great house. It made his stomach feel queasy to know that he used to be just like them—glad to be a servant for life.

That night, Miles changed the wash water for his shirt three times before it became somewhat free of blotchy dirt and sweat. He went to sleep wishing he could overhear the "gentlemen's meeting."

The next morning, the dry shirt was lying on the foot of his bed. Miles slipped it over his head while the other boys bantered back and forth like he wasn't there.

"I think I want me a shirt like that," Jacob told the rest of the boys.

"And I want mine to stink real good, too—good and strong 'nuff to walk by itself," Napoleon said, bringing laughter from the group.

"Macon," Miles said kindly, cutting into the laughter, "thank you for drying my reminding shirt."

"Let it keep on reminding you," Macon said, thinking he had helped and refusing to explain the "reminding shirt" to the nosy servants.

Miles' mind raced ahead. Macon would be giving orders soon. The boy wanted to be chosen to serve during the "gentlemen's meeting."

"I feel like workin' harder today, Macon. Can I work with you so you can train me more?" Miles continued to flatter his trainer.

"Well, I reckon I can try you out at the sideboard, Miles," Macon said, unsure but appreciating the boy's spunk. "Station yourself in the drawing room when the clock strikes three," the trainer instructed.

"When the clock strikes three," Miles parroted, realizing that he had never been assigned to the sideboard before.

He looked up to see the other boys rolling their eyes at him; he had received an assignment that should have gone to one of them. He did not care one bit.

He looked at his hands again. His palms had taken on a greenish cast from handling so many pine branches at the breaking ground. It was a good thing his shirt sleeves hid the small scars that lined his forearms.

"Servants, today we are expecting company, big company," Mrs. Bethenia said after the morning meal.

"We will take care of the creature comforts of the gentlemen who will be meeting in the great house at three o'clock." That meant small dishes and drinks would be served from the sideboard.

Macon jumped in with, "Every inch of our side of the house will be cleaned and polished. We got to tote in tables from the other side—need four servants at the door."

"How come you picked Miles for the drawing room?" Jake whined to Macon. The other boys murmured their disapproval as well.

Macon knew that the best way to keep a servant in line was not to respond to complaints. He leaned back to drain his coffee cup, silently.

Miles smiled at the ones who had been cruel to him, thinking, "What would you say if I told you I could read?"

That's what he thought about throughout the morning and afternoon while the great house was in a flurry of activity. The bell cord summoned Macon several times. Upon answering, the once calm trainer returned to them flustered by new sets of rules.

"Don't want nobody standing 'round the door when the gentlemen come," he ordered. "Mrs. Bethenia handle the door. This time, you take coats, Jake."

Jake, eager to be a part of the goings-on, asked, "Hang coats in the drawing room?"

"Don't want nobody near there. Lay the coats 'cross the settee in the sitting room," Macon said firmly.

Miles was out of practice when it came to easing around sharp corners and fine furniture pieces. He bumped into walls and left wall hangings crooked. He tripped over doorsills. Mrs. Bethenia and Macon repeatedly inspected his work and his clothing. It was of utmost importance to clean without soiling one's shirt or apron.

Around a half-hour before three o'clock, Miles was relieved when Macon sent him to fetch a fresh black string tie from the attic.

Once there, he stretched out on the bed for a brief moment to talk himself into facing Gency Tillery. "My head be so high, he see up my nose," Miles thought. "I won't look at him," he added to his thoughts as he descended the stairs.

Ol' Miss was standing outside the drawing room, talking in a low tone to Macon when Miles walked up. She wore her mixed brown and gray hair piled up, with curls extending to her shoulders.

Miles avoided their attention as best he could by looking in another direction. Judging by the din of voices, the gentlemen had been seated in the drawing room.

"Come over here, Miles," Macon called out to him, keeping a respectful distance between himself and the mistress of the house.

"Yes, sir," Miles answered like he had been trained.

"This the boy," Macon said to Ol' Miss.

Miles could tell that Macon had told her about his shirt.

"What is your name?" Ol' Miss asked like he was not supposed to have a name, but allowing him to look into her powdered, rouged face.

"Miles, Miss Tillery, ma'am."

"Macon tells me you are trying to be a good boy." She waited for him to agree.

"Yes, Mistress."

"Your Mama Cee used to be my nurse and my maid servant," the woman rattled on in the sweetest little reedy voice. "She still slack-headed?"

Miles had no answer to this question—at least not one that would keep him out of danger. He shook his head and dropped his eyes to the floor.

"Yes, ma'am, yes, ma'am," Macon said for no good reason. He bowed to Ol' Miss several times before she turned on her spool heels and entered the drawing room.

Macon blew a puff of wind out of his cheeks, relieved to be free of Ol' Miss. He looked even more relieved when she left the drawing room after whispering a few words into her husband's ear.

Soon, the trainer put a humble look on his face and entered the room. Miles followed. Ten men, including Gency Tillery, sat at the large, round table. A few logs burned in the fireplace. The sideboard was arrayed with long-stemmed glasses and balls of pastry filled with meat.

"We serve the port first," Macon said, uncorking the thick wine bottles and filling each glass halfway.

Miles did not think it odd that not one of the men acknowledged his presence when he set a small plate of food in front of each. He was careful not to brush against the men's clothing. The forks and starched white napkins were placed nearby.

"Now, gentlemen," Gency Tillery opened the discussion. "We have here, Mister Yarborough. Need I say more?" Amid the clinking wineglasses, Yarborough, a smallish man wearing a thin goatee, rose from his chair.

Miles and Macon stood at the sideboard and became

two persons who had no eyes, no ears, and no souls of their own.

"Love," a gruff voice bounced out of Yarborough's full lips. "You must teach your slaves to love you and only you." Yarborough paused and looked around. "Remind him, every chance you get, that without his love for you, he cannot survive. Do not delay punishment if a rule is broken. Develop your favorites and spies to keep you apprised of possible forthcoming treachery."

"How about the devils who burned their master's home over in Dillon?" one younger man interrupted. "What are you to do when they don't love the master? Can't rid yourself of valuable property."

"I shall address your questions at a later time," Yarborough answered the man. "Division!" he continued. "If you have not, you must draw a division line between your slaves. Recognize the importance of division and strive to keep the brutes separated. Put house servants above all others, but keep them all guessing. This way, you can keep your estate functioning smoothly."

"Plates empty," Macon spoke softly to interrupt Miles' vacant stare.

The boy balanced the platter of cold meat pastry and began to weave between the chairs, placing food on the empty plates with a silver server.

To him, the slaveholders were trying to make "fear" and "love" mean the same thing. The meeting was not telling him anything he did not know, in so many words. He returned to the sideboard and stared off again, substituting his own nonsense daydream for whatever else was said.

The noisy meeting had been in session for over an hour when Miles sensed that his face was being searched for reactions to the discussion, by Macon and by a few men.

Then when Yarborough said, "They're the ugliest of brutes and wenches of a savage race," Macon flinched like he had been stuck with a sewing needle.

The boy saw Yarborough cut his eye as Macon pretended that the back of his neck itched.

Gency Tillery called, "Boy!"

Miles calmly picked up his platter and moved toward the slaveholder, inwardly surprised that a master of the house would recognize a servant-in-training. The din ceased instantly.

"Yes, sir," Miles said, balancing the dish.

"You're new here?"

"No, sir."

"He just came back from the break—" Macon tried to help.

"What is your name?" The slaveholder shot his question.

"Miles," the boy said, trying to figure out why they pretended not to know his name. He could tell that Ol' Miss and Marse Gency knew his name as well as they knew Mama Cee. Maybe he was to be kept guessing like Yarborough had said.

"Miles what?" the master said, his slit eyes demanding.

"Miles Tillery," Miles said, using the last name he was enslaved under.

"Yes, sir, Marse Gency, sir," Macon broke in again to correct the boy.

The master switched his attention with, "You speak when spoken to, Macon!"

"Yes, sir, Marse Gency, sir," Miles corrected himself boldly, forgetting to show fear.

"What did I tell you," Yarborough spouted with conviction.

Miles wished, now, that he had paid more attention to Yarborough's speech.

"A poorly trained servant puts a house to shame," the man went on. "Soon insolence, then treachery might come to bear."

Immediately, Macon and Miles were waved out of the drawing room.

"I got nobody to blame but myself," Macon groaned on their way down the wide hall. Sweat poured down the trainer's face; they mounted the attic steps. "I was tryin' to help you, and look what you did in there."

"Didn't do nothin' but answer his questions," Miles said, feeling angry. He didn't know what made him the angriest, hearing Yarborough's meaning of love or the fact that he had forgotten to hide his true feelings, like Elijah had told him so many times.

"Didn't mean no harm," Miles apologized.

"Just you wait," Macon threatened. "Marse Gency's gonna know how I tried to train you right."

"Macon," Miles cried out like he wanted to help, "tell Marse Gency I'm not fit to be a great house servant. Tell him to make me a field hand and he won't blame you."

"You mean that?" the trainer asked, his face glowing. "Naw," Macon breathed out on second thought. "Miss Cee would . . ." He could not bring himself to finish the sentence.

Miles thought Macon hesitated because Mama Cee was old. It was unthinkable to knowingly hurt an old person. It was bad luck.

"Mama Cee will be all right," Miles assured him.

"Naw."

"Mama Cee is so glad I'm back—see, I could help her tote the water."

"Naw."

"You want to be a field hand, Macon?"

Macon groaned again. For the best part of his life, he had basked in his position of authority, his clean clothes. Some field hands bowed to him. Even the cooks and maids and butlers looked up to him. He spoke the language of Gency Tillery's great house and he could not give that up—not for Miles or his Mama Cee.

"You could help your Mama Cee out," the trainer conceded to Miles' suggestion. "Let's go," he said, heading down the attic steps.

Mrs. Bethenia told them that the men had departed.

"Tell Ol' Miss first," she advised when she heard the plan. "She'll let you see Marse Gency." Inwardly, Miles was amused when she patted his back as though comforting a child. Yet she felt that it was her duty to assist in reducing him to a field hand.

Mrs. Bethenia slipped away to pass the news to the other servants-in-training. The boys, especially Jake and Napoleon, must have been told to look at him with pity because they did. The girls forced niceties out of their mouths like, "Here's a softer dusting cloth, Miles—" and "Want me to help you tidy the drawing room, I finished my work."

To their shock, Miles smiled at each of them and thanked them for their kindness. Returning to the empty drawing room alone, he began to collect the dishes and glasses. There were four meat pastries left. He ate them and drank from the pitcher of water. He would have tasted the wine if there had been any left.

# Chapter 9

Shadows were melting away from the high-backed chairs when Macon appeared at the door.

"I tried to make him change his mind," the trainer said sadly.

"I know you did," Miles said.

"Ol' Miss went 'long with him."

"I don't hold nothing 'gainst you, Macon—understand?"

"I understand—I appreciate it too," Macon said, sounding less guilty.

"Time to eat." Mrs. Bethenia's pleasant voice made them jump. The others had gone to the servants' kitchen already, Miles guessed.

"Can I eat?" the boy asked.

"No," Mrs. Bethenia refused. "You're not a servant-in-training now."

"I say he can take somethin' with him," Macon said, looping thumbs in his suspenders. "You stand at the attic steps, boy."

It was not Mrs. Bethenia's way to challenge Macon, so her regal self floated toward the kitchen in her floor-length, calico frock. In a little while, Macon was pushing a covered, warm tin dish at him, saying, "I put 'nuff for yo' Mama Cee too."

"Thank you," Miles said, turning to leave and ignoring Macon's feigned field-hand talk.

"Wait on," Macon requested suddenly. He ran up the attic steps and returned with raggedy pantaloons and a worn, heavy coat. "You can give me your servant's clothes later," he said kindly.

Miles made his way down the back steps and into the night air. He stumbled once, forgetting about a thorny bush planted at the edge of the big yard. He passed the well, the big bell, and the paths that led to the carriage house and chicken yard and stables. Several more outbuildings stood out by themselves.

Miles knew that getting dismissed was much easier than explaining his dismissal to Mama Cee. Saying it plain was the only way he knew.

"Ol' Miss promised me!" Mama Cee shouted after hearing what had happened.

She pushed the dish of food away.

"I can get up early to help you tote the water." Miles tried to stop her from shouting, fearing they would be overheard. "I need to stay here with you."

"We got a understandin'!" Mama Cee shouted again.

Mama Cee had said something about an "understanding" before he went to the breaking ground. He picked at the dish of food.

"What kinda understandin'?"

"She know what 'tis." The old woman flopped in her

only chair, jarring the candleholder that rested on a rough-boarded table. The dim light flickered. "She know what I can do," his Mama Cee added with menace.

The boy dropped to the side of the chair and hugged her shoulders, pressing his face against her fuzzy gray hair.

"Don't want you toting them heavy buckets like that."

"Don't want you in no field," she countered.

"I have good news for you, Mama Cee."

"What is it?"

"I love you," he said, changing his mind about mentioning Elijah or reading.

"Oh hush, son; I know that," she chided him with a little laugh.

"Well, I have to keep tellin' you," Miles said, glad that he could make her feel less irritated again. It was not that he did not trust her completely. Enough was worrying her already. In time he would tell her about Elijah and freedom.

"Who first said you not fit? Macon?" She pouted.

"I said."

"You leavin' out somethin'," she accused him.

"Mama Cee, somethin' good's gonna happen to us; just you wait."

"Don't want you in no trouble."

"No trouble."

She watched him eat all of the food in the dish. Then he stretched the wire across the room so she could hang the sheet.

To save the precious candles, they talked in the pitch-dark cabin, feeling a bit of warmth from the chimney. His mattress felt more comfortable.

"They treat you bad at that breakin' ground, son?" she started out.

"No, ma'am, Mama Cee," he tried to convince her. "I met some nice folks. All of us worked hard—in the woods—trees fell down like rain, they hacked 'em down so fast. I helped cut off the limbs and all. It was near Wettown, near the water like you said."

"Bounty say it a long ways. They treat you bad at that breakin' ground, son?"

Fearing that she had become forgetful, the boy cried out in alarm, "Mama Cee, I told you . . ."

"Well, if I keep askin', you might tell me the truth." She laughed at her trickery.

Miles went on to describe the lay of the land and the red brick road. He thought he heard a faint train whistle blow before his own story put him to sleep.

The news that he had left the great house because he wanted to help his Mama Cee ran along the word-of-mouth track as fast as before. This bit of information, helped along by Mama Cee, reached every ear except the Tillerys'.

"Dere he is," some of the field hands glad-handed him while waiting for the overseer that first morning.

"I told Cee she got a fine boy," one of the women said.

"Yas'um." Miles fell into his slave talk amid the welcoming field hands. "I be glad ta see y'all," he beamed, understanding why Elijah wanted him to make friends with them.

"Work side me, Miles," a younger boy offered. "Um Dempsey. You give out, I take up de slack."

"'Preciate it, but I'ma try and keep up my own self and keep my bag full too," Miles said, thinking they would be picking cotton.

The grown folks guffawed at this and explained, "Cotton pickin' done wid. All de cotton done gone to de gin." They all hugged themselves against the November morning. "Us be pullin' corn."

Along with over fifty other field hands standing in row upon row, Miles pulled ears, one at a time, from the rustling stalks. He then tossed the ears into what Dempsey called a corncrib wagon.

"Throw over de frame," Dempsey said of the high-built wagon. A team of mules paced the end of the wagon within throwing distance if only he could pull the corn fast enough.

"Come on, Miles," Dempsey encouraged him. "Overseer busy, way over yonder. I help you out some. Dey git mean if dey think you don't keep up."

Miles took Dempsey's word that the overseers were busy with four other corncrib wagons that spanned across the rows.

No matter how fast he yanked at the ears, the other hands stayed five or six stalks ahead of him.

Three weeks went by before the acres and acres of corn-fields had been stripped clean. The ears were stored in the barns. His arm muscles ached like bad teeth.

They stored some of the stalks for the livestock to eat.

"Dis be fodder," Miles heard some field hands say for his benefit. The rest of the stalks were burned and the ashes scattered over the fields.

By the end of corn harvesting, Elijah still had not contacted him. Miles tried to push the possibility that his friend had fallen on hard times out of his mind.

"Us ain't done wid dis corn yet," Dempsey told him one evening while they were scattering the last of the ashes with wooden shovels. They headed back to join the folks at the other end of the field when the sun set.

"Ain't no mo' corn out here," Miles declared, thinking Dempsey was trying to take advantage of his ignorance.

"I know dat—it in de top of de barn, waitin'," Dempsey said. "Us gotta shuck it."

"Dat's easy," Miles said, breathing a sigh of relief.

"Us gotta shell some too, den grind some, and haul some to de mill . . ."

"I'ma tell Gency Tillery I ain't workin' no mo'." Miles drooped his lips in a pout like one of the slaveholder's grandchildren. "Who he think I is?"

This tickled Dempsey so his knees weakened.

Miles continued the act of pretending to be self-right-eous, pointing to the great house.

"Git out heah in dis field, Gency, and do dis work yo'self 'fore I whup yo' ugly behind."

At this, Dempsey fell onto the ground, kicking and howling with laughter.

Miles spotted the outline of a rider on horseback, in the shadows. Quickly he helped Dempsey to his feet. The younger boy, sensing that something was not quite right, fell silent.

"Who's there?" an overseer yelled from halfway across the field.

"Yassar, it me," Dempsey answered. "And Miles—us jest got done."

"Get to the quarters," the overseer ordered.

"Yassar," Dempsey yelled. They ran across the field to the cabins and mixed themselves into gathering wood and filling the water buckets for that night. Most of them would have time to wash the corn soot from their tired bodies. Some would show up the next morning with soot streaked on their faces and arms.

Finally, Mama Cee had accepted his field-hand status somewhat. But she kept up her steady stream of complaints against Ol' Miss with, "She know what I know." The old woman went so far as to say, "Ol' Miss wouldn't be up there in that great house if Marse Gency find out what I know." There she stopped short, despite Miles' cajoling.

After a while he advised himself, "The less I know, the better for me and Mama Cee." He had a secret too, after all.

The first of December brought freezing rain and icy winds. That did not stop the overseers from ringing the bell at dawn every day. Only they worked in the barn now.

Miles swayed Mama Cee to stay by the fire in the cabin while he toted the water and built the fire around the cauldrons. Even so, she complained, "If I can't keep movin', I ain't worth my skin. You think I'm ready to go to the grave, I reckon."

He grew silent after that, knowing she was fighting to be the boss of herself as best she could. The lines in her neck were turning to saggy folds.

"Oh, where is Elijah?" He fought to keep hoping.

The grown folks were mighty kind. He had taken a liking to Dempsey as a companion even though the boy seemed to be a year or so younger than him.

"How ol' you be, Demp?" he asked out of curiosity, while shucking corn.

"I be ten—naw—'leven," Dempsey answered, lookin' at his mama.

"Well, he come in dis worl' de year of de big snow," Dempsey's mother said.

Most of the nearby grown folks remembered the snow in question with, "It snowed up to my shoulder" or "Couldn't open de do'."

A few flurries that excited the children was about all Miles could remember.

"We gonna have us a hammer ring." Dempsey scooted

closer to tell Miles, ignoring the grown folks' stories about the snows of their childhoods. A few broke off into a song; a happy song about a girl named Lil' Lizzy.

"A hammer ring?"

"Yep," Dempsey said. "Be dere," the younger boy urged and went on to answer Miles' questioning face. "Dat's wen us be in de woods and sing and do dat ring shout. Us call it de hammer ring. Overseer ain't carin'," Dempsey assured.

Miles caught sight of one of the overseers posted at the barn door like at the breaking ground. He had forgotten about them. Meanwhile, the happy song had picked up about fifty or so voices.

*Come back, Lil' Lizzy, Come back my gal.*
*Don't you be runnin', Come back my gal.*

Corn shucks flew to the outside of the circle. Later, they could be used for stuffing mattresses and pillows.

When Miles asked Mama Cee about the hammer ring, she told him to stay away until he begged her to go with him or he would go alone.

"Field-hand foolishness," she scoffed up until that Sunday when they heard folks leaving their cabins. The air was cold even though the noonday sun burst through the cloudy sky.

The children ran toward the smoke that hung between the tall oaks and pines.

"Miss Cee!" some of the younger women squealed through their face wraps. "Ain't us glad ta see you," the one with a baby in her arms said.

"I oughta be patchin'," Mama Cee said, examining her threadbare best frock.

"No, ma'am, you needs ta be wid us," they said.

Miles ran to catch up with the young people, leaving Mama Cee to walk with the older folks. Avoiding the soot, they cut around the cornfield's edge to the fire in the woods. Miles was relieved to be out of hollering distance of the great house and the quarters. Deeply, he breathed the crisp air.

"Lay down dese shucks," the older men directed. Miles jumped to help Dempsey and a group of boys place boards on the ground, in the middle of the circle of corn shucks. The boy soaked up the friendliness of these people whom he had been taught to scorn by the great house servants. Everywhere he looked, someone was protecting a small child from the fire or making sure the olds got to choose where they wanted to sit first, nearer to the fire most of the time.

"I be so busy thinkin' 'bout dis hammer ring, couldn't git a mite of sleep last night," a woman called Pearl said to her friends.

The boy turned around and around trying to find a way to join in. He couldn't think of a thing to say; he didn't know where to sit.

"Miles!" Dempsey hollered from the other side of the

circle. "Sit right heah!" he invited, patting the shucks.

"I'ma comin'!" Miles said, searching for Dempsey in the crowd of more than a hundred. The grown folks smiled at his confusion and clapped as he ran to squeeze in beside his young friend.

Miles spotted Mama Cee, who was so tickled at seeing his shamed face her shoulders shook. He was so glad to see her laughing he forgot his self-consciousness and laughed too.

Then the crowd hushed like it was waiting for something to happen. Miles realized he was the only one glancing around. He quickly copied Dempsey's gaze, at nothing.

Presently, voices from four directions stole through the woods in a calling song. Four different tunes made up one voice that sent sadness and hope ahead of it to all of them. Miles wanted to find the voices but he dared not try.

> *Oh, sistah, what you moanin' 'bout?*
> *Listen to the hammer ringin', it's da hammer ring.*
> *Don't you hear da hammer ring?*
> *Um talkin' 'bout da hammer ringin', it's da hammer ring.*
> *Oh, brothah, what you moanin' 'bout?*
> *Don't you hear da hammer ring?*

The voices closed in on the hushed crowd. Two older men began to pound the rhythm on the boards with long sticks. The crowd swayed together.

The callers, two men and two women, emerged from

behind the bushes and trees. Their raised heads took on the look of kings and queens, never mind the field-hand garments that draped around their bodies.

The crowd answered.

*Don't you hear da hammer ring?*

For over an hour, they sang. The melancholy feeling settled in the pit of Miles' stomach. The crowd walked about, clapping and singing with two or three sets of rhythms answering at the same time. Miles tried to sing along, but the blend of the voices moved him to just sit and soak in the hope for freedom.

"Miles, I got somethin' for you," a deep, unfamiliar voice rasped in the nape of his neck. "Don't move," the voice said. "Don't look 'round."

Just then, Dempsey rushed up and flopped in front of him, showing nothing unusual on his face.

"Maybe he know the man," Miles thought to himself.

"We gonna have us de ring shout now, Miles. I let you git b'hind me," his young friend offered.

Miles groaned to himself. "I'ma see how y'all do first, den I come," he said, pointing Dempsey toward the circle of field hands, young and old. Pounding sticks sent the younger boy into a jumping rhythm as he entered the ring.

"Don't turn 'round," the voice said again. "Git to de quarters." A large hand slipped into his coat pocket.

A minute passed before Miles stood up and looked around. The stranger had melted away.

The ring shout circle had grown wider with the pounding sticks keeping a hypnotic beat to the shouting and calling songs.

He had to leave without being noticed, but there were too many people.

Slowly, he inched around the outside ring, pretending to show interest until the dance ended with shouting and clapping. That's when his offhand strides transformed to all-out running.

# Chapter 10

Not until Mama Cee's door was closed and latched did he search his pocket. His trembling fingers scooped up a tiny wad of paper that had been folded so teensy it took him a whole minute and a half to peel it open without tearing the two sheets of delicate paper.

It was a letter. Light from the sun trickled down the chimney onto Elijah's unfamiliar sprawl of joined-together letters, forming precious words. It took him some time to piece the words together.

*Dear Miles,*

*If someone observes you reading this letter, eat it. If not, burn it as soon as you finish reading. Spies are in your midst. I am well and living in one of the little houses at the breaking ground. Cobb finally purchased me. Is that not funny? Cobb purchased me. I now spend my time assisting him in selling his lumber up and down the Long-Ways Road and beyond.*

*You shall hear from me again. Study the map and learn the directions. I will add more in my next letter to you. Also, study how the words are written in this letter. Perhaps you will need to know how to write in this manner before*

*we find our way to freedom. I have been told that you are
well and that you are a field hand. Make sure you find
enough food to keep you strong.*

   *Your humble servant,*

   *E.*

*Postscript: Look for this sign on all correspondence.*

Miles traced the circled star with a faint, curvy line trailing after with his finger.

"These letters don't look right," he said to himself, trying to picture how to connect the letter *A* to *B* without looking at the paper. He wanted to learn how to connect all of the letters of the alphabet. Fear of being found out forced him to the chimney.

"I'll tell Mama Cee I made a fire for her," he thought to himself. Quickly the twirled flint stones burst the pine needles into flames. He watched the letter burn.

The labeled lines on the next sheet identified the Long-Ways Road for five miles, to the town of Tillery. Wettown was in the opposite direction. The map was marked with arrows pointing north, south, east, and west. Roads and trails like Jackson, Addleburg, and Kenyon all pointed to the north. Train stations and rivers were marked along the way too.

He burned the directions then closed his eyes and pictured the names of places.

To test his memory, he wrote some of the joined letters in the air with his finger.

"Miles, you in there?" Macon banged on the door.

"What he want?" the boy asked himself, filled with horror. For a few seconds he thought Macon could see through the door. Beads of sweat popped out on his face.

"Um in here," Miles said calmly, all the while raking pine needles and light wood into the chimney.

"Open this door," Macon said as if correcting a child.

Miles made heavy steps and lifted the door over the swollen floorboards. Macon held a wrapped dish in his hands.

"I brought you something," the trainer said, elbowing Miles out of the way to enter the cabin. "What you doing?" Macon asked, peering around and resting his eyes on the chimney.

"My fire keep on dying."

"What you makin' a fire for? You do the cookin' now?"

"Mama Cee get so cold," Miles said, seeing a hint of pity on Macon's face and not knowing what to think of it. "When she come back from that foolishness out yonder, she have a warm place."

"Well, I brought you a few mouthfuls to eat. Never did get the other dish back—clothes neither."

"Here," Miles said, exchanging the clean dish for the dish of food. He took the servant's clothes from a hook on the wall and pressed them into the trainer's hands. Then he remembered to say, "Thank you, Macon—don't know what I'd do without you."

"That's all right."

"You think you can get any old papers for me to paste over some of these cracks?" Miles nodded toward the drafty walls. Daylight was peeping between the rough boards of the poorly constructed cabin.

"I believe so—just as soon as I talk to Marse Gency."

"Ain't no need," Miles dashed out of his mouth, not wanting Gency Tillery's attention.

"We shall see," Macon insisted, as if Miles was still in training.

The boy didn't say any more. He needed to think and to worry. To his relief, Macon departed the cabin, holding the empty dish and clothing away from his pressed black cloak.

A roaring fire now swept up the chimney. Worried questions crisscrossed Miles' mind. "Did Macon see me running to the cabin? How did he know I was in here? Is he a spy? Why did he give me food?" Thinking of food, Miles uncovered the dish. Half of a baked chicken lay on a bed of buttered rice. His stomach growled at the pleasing aroma.

The noisy, jostling crowd was straggling back to the quarters.

"I sees smoke comin' out'n yo' chimney, Miss Cee," a woman's voice said.

Miles stood in the door and searched through the four o'clock sun until he saw Mama Cee, her old coat pulled up around her ears.

"I made a fire for you, Mama Cee," he yelled for all to hear.

"So nice, son," she yelled back for the same purpose.

"Wonders never cease," an older woman called Miss Cheyney chuckled. "Wisht I had me a boy lack dat."

Miss Cheyney was too far away for Mama Cee to hear the compliment but Miles saw grown folks gathering around to say nice things to her. Her face was all smiles.

Time was winding up for the field hands to frolic and visit back and forth. Preparing the evening meal was the task at hand. The next day would see them in the barn, on the ditch banks, or in the woods clearing new ground.

Mama Cee boiled collards to go along with the chicken and rice. Miles picked the bones clean. Mama Cee poured cups of the dark green collard juice for them to drink.

"Ol' folks say this is pot likker," she told Miles, pushing a cup in his hand. "Keep sickness 'way from the door."

Miles sipped the nourishing liquid. Since returning from the breaking ground he had tried many of Mama Cee's concoctions. Sassafras tea smelled the best but tasted the worst. The best tea was made from her bakerlight bushes.

"Hear them speak praise on you?" Mama asked, finishing her cup of pot likker.

"Yes, ma'am," he answered modestly, knowing how she felt about self-bragging. Yet she allowed herself to boast about him to anyone who had an ear.

"Well, they know I got me a good boy."

Miles wondered what her life was like before he became her boy. Was she always alone? He tried to picture her without wrinkles and gray hair.

Other field hands, young and old, looked after their weaker relatives. The olds whose children had been sold away were seen to by anyone who happened to be nearby. His Mama Cee had him. He wished he had told Elijah about her at the breaking ground, but he knew he would have dissolved into a puddle of tears if he had called her name. He wondered if he would ever understand breaking ground fear.

He felt guilty about deceiving those who thought he was special because he let go of a "good p'sition" to become a field hand for the sake of Mama Cee. "Not all true," he thought that night on his mattress. "Wish I could say why."

"Trust no one," Elijah had said. "Spies are in your midst."

In his heart of hearts he knew Elijah was right. Sooner or later, though, Mama Cee would have to be told. "How can I tell Elijah 'bout her?" he anguished. "I can't go to freedom unless Mama Cee is with me. Mayhap he'll tell me how to send him a letter."

He closed his eyes and pictured the circled star and the arrows pointing north, south, east, and west. It was like viewing a little piece of the whole wide world.

He rubbed at the burning sensation in his temples. Excitement.

Slowly, peaceful sleep stretched him out, his head cradled in the crook of his arm.

Two weeks had passed since the hammer ring, and field hands were finishing the shucking in the barn. Elijah had not made contact with him again.

From time to time Miles caught himself studying the faces of the grownups. Any one of the men could have slipped the letter into his pocket. If only it had been possible for him to keep the letter a little longer, just so he could have a touchable thing nearby for comfort, like Nero's shirt.

One day, Miles saw an overseer disappear from the loft to spy on the men in the field. There were two of them. He learned they were called "Seer" and "Overseer" behind their backs. This one did most of his talking with the whip— Mister Davidson. McCain, the older one, was just as sneaky and mean.

Davidson and McCain tried to make themselves appear to be everywhere, all the time watching. The overseers thought the field hands were too simple to catch on to this trick.

Knowing they had a little time before McCain could creep up on them, Miles stood, stretched his legs, and looked around.

"Y'all look dere!" he called out.

From overhead in the loft, a few of the younger field hands came and gazed at the rich teams of horses that pulled shiny, traveling coaches up the driveway of the great house.

"Whole drove of 'em," they marveled at the horse-drawn coaches. They could not have seen this sight from the quarters.

"Dey gonna have a high ol' time," Miles said, remembering the scented pine boughs and red ribbons and the music at the ballroom.

Christmas greetings had lit up the happy faces when he held the door for guests that carried beautifully wrapped packages. The guests sauntered across the polished floors and draped themselves over cushioned chairs. Not even the servants were allowed to take part in what Macon and Mrs. Bethenia called "white folks' Christmas."

"Don't you want ta go back?" Dempsey's mama teased, like he was missing special treats.

"What for?" Miles asked. "Servants jest serve all day and all night. Dey ain't let them have nothin' ta do wid no Christmas. Dat company be dere 'til January, and Ol' Gency and Ol' Miss be calling on servants ta wait on 'em," he said bitterly. The group eyed him, unbelieving.

"How 'bout dem gussied-up britches you was all togged down in?" Dempsey challenged. "You be up dere eatin' cakes and pies and sech."

Miles laughed and led them back to shucking corn. If only he could tell Dempsey, "That person is no more. I would rather be free than eat cakes and pies and wear fine clothes." But he couldn't tell his smiling friend without giving himself away.

Dempsey's mother broke out in a corn shucking song. Miles was one of the first ones to pick up the rhythm. He liked the deep tone of her voice. The others dropped in at the bottom of the song, a kind of song Gency Tillery did not mind them singing.

*Gotta shuck dis corn dis mornin', shuck dis corn.*
*Gotta shuck dis corn 'til night, shuck dis corn.*
*Shuck with all my might, shuck dis corn,*
*Shuck dis corn, shuck dis corn.*

Miles began to hum the catchy tune. He guessed the hammer ring and other songs were the field hands' way of finding something to be happy about, like the white folks' Christmas. He didn't know why the singing and shouting made him feel happy and sad at the same time, but it did.

"Us think right smart of you down here wid us—white folks ain't everything," Dempsey's mama said, after ending the song. He suspected that she wanted him to further criticize his days at the great house.

"Certainly so" and "ain't dat da truth" trickled out from the grown folks. Their smooth faces pointed toward him and waited for juicy gossip to drip from his lips. He glanced around, hoping to see the overseer.

"Spies in your midst," Elijah had said.

The back of his neck tingled with suspicion, yet he could not risk bringing shame on Mama Cee by ignoring grown folks.

"I ruther be down here wid y'all," he decided on, sweetly, knowing he had already talked too much.

"Where are you, Elijah?" he thought to himself. "I got a big mouth." His complaints had been to show Dempsey that a great house servant was a slave the same as a field hand. But he had talked himself up a tree.

Just then, the overseer sneaked into the loft. All hands sensed his presence and shucked corn at a frenzied pace. The mouths reopened the corn shucking song.

Miles had never been so glad to see nightfall.

The morning after the field hands finished the corn, mid-January, the ground was coated with ice and sleet. Chills and fever came to the quarters. Hacking coughs and sneezes escaped through the cabin doors.

Miles had spent the night keeping a small fire going in the chimney. He didn't think Mama Cee's thin blanket was enough to keep her warm. She refused his blanket.

He bound his feet with burlap bags to keep from slipping on the icy ground and made his way to the well by the time the first bell rang. Every cabin housed four or more sick people. Friends and relatives skidded between the cabins looking for root medicine or advice.

"Curse your lazy black hearts to the devil. Get to clearing that new ground," Miles heard the overseer yell to the bedridden folks after the second bell had rung. All the while his whip cracked. Quiet groans tore out of the cabins.

Believing the overseer did not understand, Miles left the group of about thirty that seemed well enough to work.

"Mayhap I tell him what de matter," he said over his shoulder to the astonished group.

The boy came across Davidson in a cabin near the nursery. "Dey sick wid the fever," he rushed in and told the overseer.

In a flash the whip was aimed at him, but the overseer was standing too close for Miles to receive the full strength of the lick. Quickly, he cushioned himself by stepping in closer to the man's limited arm swing.

"Why you hit me?" Miles cried out. "Dey sick!"

"Leave my boy be!" Miles heard Mama Cee shout. She skidded out of the nursery, still shouting, "Don't you hit my boy," like she had lost her mind. "You not suppose to hit my boy."

She grabbed the whip's end and shrieked, "This camp's 'bout overrun with dead field hands! Can't you see they sick? They dying of the galloping fever!"

The overseer glared in shock at the old woman. In all of his twelve years on the Tillery Plantation not one slave had ever fought back.

"Leave go, you old wench!" he sneered, yanking the whip and making a fist of his free hand to knock her upside the head. The old woman held on to the end of the whip.

Miles wedged between the overseer and his Mama Cee. He grabbed her arm and peeled her strong fingers from around the whip.

"Mama Cee, my baby dyin'!" a man cried out, grabbing her from behind. She was snatched out of Miles' grasp;

at the same time a burning pain lapped around his upper body. The snapping sound stung his ears. He fell onto the ground and rolled away from the overseer.

Davidson let the whip swing again.

A crowd of field hands gathered. Miles heard people running and shouting to each other as if desperate noise would save them and him from harm.

"Git Marse Gency," they wailed. "Git Marse Gency— Ol' Amos done died!"

The boy lay on the ground, holding his stinging back to the cold ground. The overseer coiled his whip and picked his way toward the great house.

No one went to the field that day. The boy was glad he had taken the licks instead of Mama Cee even though his back burned like fire. He stood in Mama Cee's door, telling folks the overseer had not hurt him much. They soon shied away to first one cabin, then the other.

Miles' back felt sticky from sweat or blood or both, but he did not bother to take his shirts off. To keep from wishing for Elijah, he toted wood and laid it at the doors of the sick cabins.

Ol' Miss sent Davidson back with a quart jar of black fever pills and asafetida cloves to wrap in a pouch and suspend around the neck.

"Swallow one anyhow," the overseer ordered those who had not developed a fever. Miles pretended to swallow the pill. Then he spat it in the chimney. The odor of asafetida cloves reeked throughout the quarters.

"Mama Cee, I ain't got the fever," Miles protested after she looped the homemade pouch around his neck.

"Keep it next to your heart," she urged, ignoring his complaints and pulling aside his shirt to check every evening.

"How 'bout if I drop it in my pocket?" he asked, thinking of throwing the pouch in the bushes. She would have none of that.

The pill, if it could have helped, was too late for some in the quarters. Within three days, three women, one man, and two young babies were taken "feet foremost" out of the cabins to a frozen burial ground—most of their kin too sick to grieve.

The raging fever so alarmed Gency Tillery that he sent for Dr. McPherson. Just before noon on the third day, Miles watched the doctor clump in and out of the drafty cabins, spending a little time in some and walking out of others as soon as he walked in.

The winter sun and constant footsteps chipped and melted much of the ice. Soon sticky mud clung to heavy shoes and boots.

"Should have requested my services earlier," the doctor fussed to the overseer, leaving the cabin where Dempsey lived with his papa, mama, and seven brothers and sisters. Dempsey was the youngest.

"Mister Tillery stands to lose more valuable property," Miles heard the doctor say.

Not wanting to hear more terrible news, Miles backed

himself into his Mama Cee's cabin and closed the door, losing daylight. A fire smoldered in the chimney. She was still in the nursery, taking care of sick babies. He stumbled to his mattress, fell, and buried his face in the crook of his arm. The rustle of corn shucks blocked some of the outside noise.

A woman screamed, "My po' baby!" It sounded like Dempsey's mother.

"Please don't get sick, Mama Cee," Miles moaned out loud. "Don't get sick ... don't get sick ..." He didn't know he had fallen asleep until someone tugged at his arm.

"Wake up," the familiar voice rasped, folding the boy's fingers over a small wad of paper. "Don't look at me," the voice cautioned.

By instinct Miles gaped in the direction of the voice. He saw only a brief shadow stealing between the cracks of light from two opposite walls. Quickly, he sealed his eyes.

Within a few seconds the door closed noiselessly behind the figure. It was quiet outside the cabin when he unfolded the paper by candlelight. The circled star with the faint line was at the top of the page this time. Elijah's familiar penmanship invited him to read.

> *Good news, Miles,*
> *Have planned the complete route to freedom.*
> *Will take more time to carry out than I had thought.*
> *Find a way to practice writing. I know you can.*

*Know you have sickness there.*

*Eat all you can, whenever you can. Keep up your strength and patience.*

*Study map.*

*Humble Servant,*

*E.*

Miles was really worried now. He had no way of getting in touch with Elijah. How could he tell his friend about Mama Cee? He laid the paper on the fire a few minutes later, having added the latest part of the map to his memory. Vaguely, he remembered seeing a man at the train station with a feather and small bottle of dark liquid called ink. He wished he had watched more closely. The ground was too frozen for him to practice writing in the dirt. Plus, someone would surely see him. He had to find another way.

A slight smile accompanied his next thought. "Elijah didn't say nothin' 'bout me burnin' his letter dis time. He 'pect I know what ta do."

Slave talk was comforting, even in his thoughts. The words were simple but meant so much. He felt at home while watching how the field hands acted and listening to their subtle, double-meaning words. In a way, he was learning as much from them as he had from Elijah.

"Come and get it! Come and get it!" came a loud booming voice. Miles jumped again.

"Come and get it!" Macon said again.

Miles pulled the door open. The trainer was bending over bundles of old newspapers.

"Flour paste this over the cracks and over the door," Macon said. "Keep the draft out. Marse Gency said so."

Immediately, Miles became suspicious. Surely Macon was spying on him and whoever had delivered Elijah's letters.

Macon slapped the paper in Miles' arm for Mama Cee and gave some to other folks who lived in cabins with babies and old folks. His unconcerned face told Miles nothing.

In the cabin, Miles could see that the papers had been cut into mismatched strips so as to make it difficult to read a continuing sentence. He called out individual words to himself.

"I b'lieve I can practice writin' on the edges," he thought, pressing the papers on the chair's bottom. Then all of a sudden Dempsey ran across his mind, and the woman's cry. He felt lonely and tired. "Oh, Dempsey," he moaned. "Was dat yo' mama cryin' for you?"

"Bring something out here for this flour, boy," Macon yelled through the door.

"Ain't got nothin' but dis," Miles said, opening the door and walking out with the servant's dish. The woman called Pearl held out a cracked bowl.

"You seen Dempsey?" Miles asked her quietly. "He sick too?"

"Naw, he ain't sick. Dere he is." She pointed toward a cabin.

Miles dropped the dish and ran, yelling, "Dempsey! I thought you was gone."

"Gone whar?" Dempsey laughed out, stepping out of the door, holding on to his family's skillet.

"Come back here and get this flour, boy. What's the matter with you?" Macon scolded.

"Nothin', nothin'," Miles said over his shoulder as tears ran down his face.

That's when the younger boy realized that "gone" meant "dead." At the thought of his own death, Dempsey started crying for himself and the others that had died.

"Stop that foolishness," Macon said sharply. The boys did not stop. And Macon was more confused when Dempsey's sister saw them crying and she began to cry. A few of the grown folks, men too, stood in the doorways and softly joined in the crying.

Gency Tillery and Ol' Miss appeared, covering their mouths and noses with handkerchiefs. No one seemed frightened to see them peering around to make sure that everything was being done to save their property.

"How many dead?" he asked the overseer.

"Six died of the fever, Mister Tillery, sir," the overseer spouted as if clearing himself of blame.

"Add a bit more to the ration and don't ring the bell 'til you hear from me," the slaveholder directed while Macon stood at attention and copied them now with his hand over his mouth.

"Yes, sir, Mister Tillery, sir." The overseer nodded and stepped away from the cabins to follow his superior out of the quarters.

At last, Macon doled out the rest of the flour. Quickly, he threw the empty flour sack aside and left the quarters as fast as his feet could carry him. Miles picked up the cloth sack and rolled it under his arm; it could be useful one day.

Mama Cee had heard about the outbreak of crying by the time she returned from nursing sick children whose mothers had come down with the fever.

"All y'all needed to be washed clean the same as me," she said of the tears.

"Yes, ma'am," Miles piped in quickly. He laid more wood on the fire and told her about the newspaper and flour, pushing the flour sack under her bed to rest among other bits and pieces of things.

# Chapter 11

On the fifth fever day, Mama Cee was a welcome sight to Miles when she entered the cabin, tired but not sick-looking.

"Us ain't git the fever," he said as she sat by the fire. "Hope us don't neither." Miles pretended not to notice Mama Cee's puzzled stare. "Ain't nobody say nothin' 'bout me toting water up dere," he went on.

"Son," she said calmly. "I been listenin' to you. You're commencin' to talk more and more like a field hand. Why is that so?"

"I am a field hand," he joked.

"Now, son." She used her scolding tone, exasperated.

"Mama Cee, I can talk as well as Gency Tillery if I'd like to," he cut in quickly.

"You used to talk better," she said.

"Mama Cee, I can read," Miles said matter-of-factly.

"Don't say that!" she hissed.

The boy bowed his head. The timing was ripe. He was glad he had told her. "Folks dying in the quarters," he mused. He reasoned that if ever they separated from each other she would know his secret. He could read. He wanted her to be proud of him right then, like in his dreams at the breaking ground.

"Who showed you readin'?" she pitched forward and whispered, believing him, her face showing fear and excitement.

"Elijah," Miles said just as softly, planning to leave out parts of information about Elijah for then. "He be at the breakin' ground. Nobody else found out he could read."

"I know you are smart." She leaned back in wonder. "You could piece together things about living at three, four years old. You could remember any and everything."

"I can write too, Mama Cee," Miles added.

She gawked at him.

"Mama Cee, Elijah gave me writing lessons too," he said, filling in the gap.

"Hush, son, b'fore I brag myself to death to myself," she laughed and wrapped her arms around her shoulders. Her rocking from side to side reminded him of the dancing moves in the ring shout. She was dancing to a song in her head.

Miles raised himself up and began to peel the sweet potatoes. They had real meat too now, instead of just pork skins. He laid four slices of pork in the iron skillet and nestled the pan among the hot coals.

"We got collards left over from last night," she said after a while.

They had the same meal the next morning without the collards. After thinking about it for two days, she made Macon's flour into bread for sopping blackstrap molasses.

Tired of cornmeal, all of the field hands made bread with the flour instead of using it to paste newspaper over the cracks in the walls. Miles hid Mama Cee's paper under his mattress.

By the end of January, Dr. McPherson took credit for healing the last few sick folks in the quarters with his doses of caramel. Seventy-five or so had been stricken with the fever. Eight more had died since the outbreak. Recovering men, women, and children looked out of raw-boned faces with glassy eyes. They moved slowly, eating little.

No one spoke of Bounty. Miles saw him entering the stables one evening. He did not seem to be sick. The boy guessed that the old man slept near the horses—somewhere.

Miles did not know why some field hands had died and some had not. The doctor had treated them all the same. Why some of them did not come down with the fever at all, like himself and Mama Cee, was a mystery to him. He suspected the doctor didn't know the answer to this question either.

"I have brought them through," the doctor contended to the overseers. All the while he stuffed his medicines in a black leather bag, preparing to end his visits in the quarters. "I shall tell the master they could do with rest now."

Miles thought Miss Cheyney, who had almost died, made the most sense when she proclaimed, "Dat doctah ain't heal us. He ain't kill no fever either. Dat fever wore out from us fightin' it, dat's all. It jest got tired, fightin' us back—den it limped on out dese quarters. Bet it be havin' a high ol' time somewhere else right now."

The bell resumed its stabbing claps one morning after the ice had melted. Underfoot, the ground was mushy and cold, as usual for the second week of February in South Carolina.

The stronger field hands returned to the woods where at least five acres of stumps and timber trees waited to be cleared before spring planting.

Every so often, Miles told Mama Cee a bit more information about Elijah.

One night in the cabin, he sat at her feet and whispered to her about Nero's burial. He pulled up his layers of bedraggled shirts to show her Nero's shirt next to his skin.

"You left out a lot when I asked you about that breakin' ground," she whispered back, with tears in her eyes.

"Ain't no need to cry, Mama Cee. Can't you see I'm all right?" he tried to console her. He meant to get her ready for the next step by telling these things. It was going on time for him to start the task of getting them free.

"That poor boy died," she choked out. "It coulda been you, son."

Miles slipped off his shoe and began a steady tapping on the floor with the heel of it, making their words unclear to anyone who might be listening outside.

Then he blurted out in a whisper, "Mama Cee, Elijah's gonna help us find the way to freedom."

"'How...when...what you mean?" she babbled, stunned.

"When time come," he said.

"They send dogs——" she started to say.

"We ain't gonna run, we gonna take time and plan——"

"Don't say nothin' else!" she warned him, nodding toward the outside wall.

He didn't stop tapping the heel of his shoe. She didn't complain about the noise. The steady beat released some of the pressure that had been building up in his neck and back. Mama Cee relaxed a little too.

"I want you to come with me to freedom, Mama Cee," he said.

"I can't go, too old," she said to the rhythm of his tapping.

"Can't go by myself, too young," he countered.

With that, she snickered and covered her mouth to keep from laughing out loud.

"You going to manhood," she told him, keeping to the beat.

"A man looks out for his mama."

"Reckon I'll try to go," she said, slowing down and studying his face.

The beat stopped. He stood up, feeling ten feet tall and that he had lived much longer than twelve years.

"Well," she said, "I reckon I will go."

"I already know that," he said kindly.

Elijah trusted him. She trusted him. The three of them

made a coming-together circle in his mind. For the first time in his life he felt that he was on his way to becoming a man. He urged Mama Cee to save her strength for freedom-going.

Sometimes Miles would meet Bounty, the silent runaway tracker who still kindled the fires in the great house fireplaces. Miles found out the old man spent the rest of his day in the woodshed, cutting thin wood slats for kindling and searching among the fallen trees for fast-burning light wood.

"How you be, Mister Bounty?" Miles spoke to the old man one morning.

"Uh-huh," Bounty grunted with his head down. That was all.

Sometimes, the hands were startled by the presence of Gency Tillery watching them from a distance at the edge of the quarters and at the edge of the woods.

"Marse Gency either scared some more of us will lay down and die on him, or he mad because we're not workin' hard enough," Mama Cee said one night in the cabin. "You seen how he watches us like a chicken hawk."

"Davidson tell me ta work in the stables today and I ain't been sick," Miles told her. He did not say that he felt that somebody was watching him too.

"That's good, son. That work is easy," Mama Cee told him. "Keep up your strength too." She tugged at the hanging sheet. "Get ready and lay yourself down, son," she urged.

Miles slipped off his muddy shoes. He could not understand why the overseer, who clearly hated him, had assigned him easy work. He wouldn't have anything to do but feed and rub down horses. It was like they wanted him to be alone so he could be watched.

Poor Dempsey had to dig stumps, one of the most hated jobs and the most backbreaking for someone so young. Miles missed his laughing and joking new friend who now walked about slumped in a daze.

Miles lowered his weary body down. The rustling shucks brushed past his ear. Now he could think—about nothing but horses and freedom.

Miles liked horses. He especially liked Big Red, a riding horse Ol' Miss's company rode when he was a servant-in-training.

He looked forward to morning, tracing his steps past the well, the carriage house, and poultry yard to the stables. Instantly, his mind backed up to chickens and feathers.

"Mama Cee," he called gently.

"What, Miles," she answered, her tone tinged with sleep.

"You know anythin' 'bout ink so I can write?"

"Yes, tomorrow," she said from a doze.

The next evening Miles put himself in the thick of a flock of white chickens. He ran his eyes over the ground for loose feathers. Sure enough, he found a few and rammed them between his shirts. He wished he had thought of this before.

At the end of the day, Mama Cee entered the cabin with an apron gathered into a sack of lumpy somethings and a sly grin on her face.

"Git dat kettle on de fire, boy," she said in field-hand talk.

Miles smiled. "What you got, Mama Cee?" he asked, feeling the hard lumps as she inched to the table with the same grin.

"Ink," she said, grabbing a handful of black walnuts out of her apron.

"Ink? Dese ain't nothin' but walnuts."

"I knows it, but us gonna make ink," she bristled.

"You gonna boil the color out," he said, examining a black walnut that stained his hand.

He dropped in as many walnuts as the kettle of water would hold.

She dipped the old walnuts out of the boiling water and added fresh ones three or four times to the same water. In the end, the jet-black water had thickened and measured to a half-pint of "ink."

Miles gingerly poked his fingertip in the ink after the evening meal. It was cool to the touch.

"Dis how dey done it when I was in the great house," Mama Cee told him, angling the cut of a large feather with her knife. "Try it, son," she rushed, holding the kettle and puffing with excitement.

He dipped the feather into the liquid and let the excess ink drop off. Carefully, he scribbled two words on the edge of the newspaper. Then he stood back to let her see what he had written.

"Mama Cee," he said.

"What?" she answered, peering at the paper.

"That's what it says—'Mama Cee.'"

"Oh, son, my real name Caroline—write dat."

She had never told him her real name.

Even more carefully, he wrote *Caroline*.

Wordlessly, she studied her name, holding the paper upside down and right side up in the candlelight. Curly lines joined together to form a name she had not often heard. She had never before seen her name in writing.

"I wonder if I be able to know it again," she said to herself and laid the paper across the hot coals.

The boy stepped back and watched the bright flame dance. He dumped the used walnuts in the fire and hid the kettle of "ink" under her bed.

"Dat be used ta put color in clothes too," she said, offering a way to protect themselves if someone asked. "Us use gooseberries and pokeberries too."

Miles tossed the used feather in the chimney. She buried the stems of the unused feathers around the band of an old straw hat. He tossed the hat under the table.

"Dat good, son—dey won't know a thing 'bout us business," she smirked.

Miles knew why she had spoken in field-hand talk. The very rhythm of it made her want freedom more than ever.

He smiled at her. Mama Cee had never been to the breaking ground but in a way, she had been broken. He hoped that the thought of freedom would put her back together too.

For a while longer, the folks who had gotten over the fever were given as many sheltered jobs as possible, like helping the cobblers, meat smokers, and wheelwrights. Still no one was assigned to work in the stables with Miles. He did not know what had happened to the boy who worked there before him.

March rolled around blustery and sunshiny. Folks in the quarters still chased away chilly mornings and evenings by maintaining a small fire in the chimney.

Macon showed up two more times, the first time to bring cast-off clothes to him and Mama Cee.

The second time Miles was alone when Macon arrived, smacking his lips. "I be toting a dish of chicken and gravy, bread, made wid flour mind you, and dis jar of peach preserves," the trainer announced, bowing low.

"Why you bring me dis?" Miles inquired, in spite of his appetite for food other than sweet potatoes, collards, and salt pork. He stood in the doorway, keeping Macon out of the cabin.

"Told you before," Macon crooned. "I 'preciate how you 'greed to come back down here in dese nasty quarters."

Macon's field-hand talk sounded like mockery to Miles. The boy pretended not to notice that Macon wanted something very badly.

"Thank you, Macon," Miles said politely, reaching for the dish.

"Well, I wants to talk wid you 'bout somethin' too." Macon advanced, raising his foot to enter the cabin.

The trainer's shifty eyes seemed to know that Mama Cee was late leaving the nursery. Miles stepped aside.

"Ain't you got no candle?" Macon asked, standing inside the dark cabin.

Miles pulled a shaft of straw from the broom and let it catch fire from the chimney. Soon the candle glowed.

Right away, Macon's eyes flickered from one corner of the cabin to the next. From floor to ceiling, his eyes ran over the four walls.

"What you tryin' ta find?" Miles asked, wondering what Macon's excuse would be this time.

"Why didn't you flour paste the paper over the cracks?" he asked.

That surprised Miles. He had long since forgotten how everyone in the quarters used the flour.

He admitted, "We made bread wid it, long time ago."

"What you do with the paper—kindle fire?"

"Yes," Miles said, pulling his eyes in the opposite direction of his mattress.

Macon picked up the candle, held it high, and scanned the ceiling more closely. The trainer kept cutting his eyes at Miles.

"What you lookin' for, now?" Miles asked, not showing suspicion or guilt.

"Tryin' ta see how you be livin', boy. I think I can help you and Miss Cee out."

"Us livin' fine," Miles said, pondering why Macon hadn't searched the cabin while he and Mama Cee were away all day. The trainer would have had daylight on his side and he would not have had to worry with food. Then again, maybe he had and could not find whatever he was searching for.

Just then, Mama Cee pushed on the door.

In a twinkling, Macon shoved the candle at Miles.

"I brung you somethin' good to gnaw on, Miss Cee," Macon prattled, showing all of his teeth, trying to make her feel comfortable.

"How are you faring today, Mister Macon?" Mama Cee asked.

Macon, taken aback, had forgotten that Mama Cee had been a great house servant before he became a trainer. She would never speak in field-hand talk to him.

He sputtered out, "Fine, yes indeed, fine. Hope you enjoy the dish."

She noticed the dish and thanked him in rapid succession many times over. Now walking toward him, she said, "Thanky, thanky," a few more times.

He backed out of the door, accepting her thanks with his head nodding and his lips telling her how glad he was to help out.

"I believe you thanked him into bad health," Miles chuckled after he closed the door behind Macon.

"He ought to be—coming down here like somebody's

high-stepping horse." Mama Cee scowled in the direction of the great house. "What did he want?"

Miles told her how Macon had behaved, searching around and all, in the ceiling and the corners of the cabin.

"He will never find it!" she burst out.

The boy did not bother to ask what. He had to leave the secret with her. But now it was as plain to him as the horses in the stables. Macon was a spy for Ol' Miss.

Mama Cee put a look of utmost satisfaction on her face as they sat down and supped on the delicious chicken and gravy.

"Don't sop gravy," she fussed at him. "Spread it on the bread, then eat."

"I'll 'member dat 'nother time," he teased, soaking the soft bread in the thick gravy and stuffing it in his mouth. He pulled the tender chicken from the bone with his fingers. Macon had dished out enough for three people. Miles and Mama Cee ate it all that night.

"Put back some preserves for another time," she cautioned, after Miles dug deep into the small jar of golden sweetness with his wooden spoon.

Before he pinched out the candle, Miles pulled up his sleeves and pumped his growing arm muscles. He had slit his shoes to give his growing feet more room.

He wished he could see himself in a looking glass. None were allowed in the quarters. He could see that he was almost as tall as Mama Cee.

Yes, he was eating all he could and keeping his strength up too. Elijah would be glad to see him. If only Elijah would contact him again.

"When, Elijah, when?" he lay on his mattress and asked the dark room.

# Chapter 12

By the middle of March, the last of the feverish folks were back to their usual work. It was time for plowing the fields and for spring planting. Sickness had delayed the new ground and the overseers drove harder to make up for lost time.

Yet Miles remained in the stables. The livery hands talked to him a few times when they wanted his help in polishing the carriages. But no matter how closely he watched them, he could read nothing on their faces.

Then, one morning after he had toted the water and built the fire around the cauldrons, he found himself among a group of field hands who had stirred themselves into a puddle of misery because it was day break and the first bell had not yet rung. Instead of resting, they paced between cabins, speculating on possible news. The hated bell gave them no pleasure, but the lack of the sound gave them less.

"Death in de big house only thang stop dat bell," Miss Cheyney announced as if she held this knowledge in the palm of her hand.

"Somebody up dere dead," the boy heard from outside Mama Cee's door. They knew if the slaveholder were to die, families would likely be split up among heirs or sold off somewhere.

"Dey gonna sell some o' us off," became the cry that went from cabin to cabin.

Mama Cee whispered to him, "If it ain't Ol' Miss, you and me will be all right."

Miles stole back to the well, looking for the washwomen.

"Mayhap dey know what wrong," he breathed out loud. The water cauldrons were sending steam into the misty air. No one was in sight. Suddenly, he twisted toward hoof beats coming from the stables.

Gency Tillery was riding Big Red straight toward him. Davidson and McCain followed on two plug horses.

Miles dared himself to stand still and face the oncoming riders.

"Get your simple-minded self to the quarters," McCain yelled as they rode by, narrowly missing him. He looked at where the horses had kicked back clods of soft dirt on his feet.

The clanging bell gathered the hands to their usual spot at the edge of the quarters as he ran to take a space in the middle of the group. Mama Cee and the other olds waited in the nursery. Miles was startled to see Bounty creep between the cabins and stand with them.

Gency Tillery sat motionless on Big Red, turning his head ever so slightly to observe a particular field hand or another. All eyes were cast down.

"You lazy, good-for-nothing gals, get your babies and tell them old buzzards your master wants all of you here,"

Davidson snarled, stabbing downward with his finger.

The women with babies bumped about among the crowd, clearing way, and running to retrieve their children. None of them had the time to wonder what was about to happen.

Miles saw that Mama Cee was the last to leave the nursery. She looked lost and tired. He wanted to go to her but settled on not bringing attention to himself or her.

"Shadup!" McCain yelled, even though the crowd was engulfed in silence.

"Your past sickness has cost me time and money," Gency Tillery began to speak. "So from now on you will work a half day on Sunday. From now on there will be no more nursery. Take your children to the field with you. From now on, I will carry no more dead weight. Those who have tended babies or sat idle doing much of nothing will live elsewhere. Sheds will be built for you by tomorrow, near the bottom, on the far side of the plantation. Whoever wishes to give you food or give you water may do so, but not on my time—on your time."

The hands mumbled among themselves. Miles pretended to be mumbling too as he met Mama Cee's eyes. She showed no feelings. That was good, he thought.

The master paused and hunted for mumbling individuals. McCain spat, "Shadup!"

The master continued with, "From now on, you must let Mister McCain and Mister Davidson know if you see any strangers on my plantation, black or white. The one who brings news will receive a gold piece and a whole day off to spend it, however he or she chooses, in town."

Without another word from Gency Tillery, Miles watched Big Red swing, as if on wheels, and trot the slave-holder toward the Long-Ways Road.

The overseers led the others to the field, singing the "Lil' Lizzy" song.

Numb, Miles let his feet take him to the stables. He looked back to see Bounty trailing after him.

"Dey makin' you go to the woods too, Mister Bounty?" Miles waited to ask, hoping the old man would talk to him. He had never thanked Bounty for bringing the message to Mama Cee.

"I be heah long-o," Bounty snapped. "Too long-o. Shoulda been gone."

They walked on together. At the stables the old man waved and continued on with his head down.

Wearily, the boy entered the stall of fresh hay, feeling, for sure, that someone had been watching him. "Mayhap dey seen me git dem feathers too." The worries entered his head like little pegs pounding his temples. Only a deep intake of air relieved the throbbing. Slowly, he wrapped his hand around his pitchfork and sank its prongs into the stack of hay.

"Careful," said a squeaky voice.

"Naw!" the boy protested, stepping back.

"Quiet!" the voice hissed.

Speechless, Miles gaped at the quaking hay. Before his eyes, Elijah emerged, grinning, one hand motioning for quiet and extending a glad hand.

Miles clasped the hand and wouldn't let go. His friend didn't seem to mind.

"I don't have much time," Elijah said calmly.

Miles butted in, "Elijah, I got to tell you 'bout Mama Cee."

"I know about your Mama Cee and the old folks too," his friend told him. "I understand you can't leave her. There's been trouble. After this day you will not see me until you get to freedom."

"Why?"

"Someone has betrayed us. Take this bottle of ink and this paper."

"Who?" Miles asked, sliding the folded paper between his shirts.

"I don't know for sure," Elijah whispered, "but tomorrow, when he returns, Cobb will find out about me and what I've been doing. So I had to escape and get to you before word gets here to Gency Tillery.

"Here are the maps and directions and instructions," Elijah offered, stuffing four tiny wads of paper in Miles' pocket. "There is a spy here on this plantation too. If they find these papers—"

"I will be careful," Miles blurted out, nodding his head.

A horse neighed loudly, shattering the quiet.

"Go to the horses!" Elijah whispered urgently.

Miles tore down the narrow, twenty-foot aisle to the horses' stalls. His nimble fingers shook the last bag of oats into their bins. The horses quieted down. He rushed back to Elijah.

"Boun-ty," his friend whispered, melting behind a stack of hay.

"What about Bounty?" Miles wanted to shout.

The stable door squeaked. Miles looked in the opposite direction of Elijah's rushing footsteps.

"What you waitin' on, Miles?" one of the livery hands whined, looking around. Miles did not know the young man's name or what he was talking about so he just answered, "Nothin'."

"I gotta harness Pat and Jerry for Marse Gency's lil' grands, and you ain't finished feeding 'em yet," the livery hand complained.

"Horses be ready d'rectly," Miles said, not looking at the man and digging a pitchfork full of hay. "Marse Gency been talkin' ta us—dat's why dey ain't fed."

"Well, git a move on you."

"Be ready d'rectly," Miles said again, slowly leveling the hay to the horses. The horses craned their heads around to see him. This calmed his nerves.

The livery hand sucked his teeth at Miles before taking rankled steps out of the stables.

A while later, the sound of laughing and squealing children cut into his thoughts. He supposed they were riding Pat and Jerry, the three-year-old, yellowish horses. Miles quickly read the instructions. Question after question wrapped around his head. If only Elijah had had the time to explain more. Was Bounty a spy? No, he couldn't be. Gency Tillery was sending the old man to the woods too. Was he supposed to ask Bounty to help him to freedom? Could it be that the mean slave tracker would help him escape? An image of the old man singing a message to Mama Cee softened the boy's heart.

The echo of hammers answering one another let him know that Gency Tillery's plan to move the old folks to the edge of the woods was being carried out. Miles put the maps back into his pocket after studying the difficult details.

After the children grew tired of riding he would rub the gentle animals down. Big Red would need a rubdown too—as soon as Gency Tillery returned. To Miles, horses were as gentle as they were big.

To rest his edgy nerves, he daydreamed of a horse of his own—a horse like Big Red. He drifted out of one daydream and into another. That's what he did when he was worried sometimes.

"Dey say Mist' Bounty sleep somewhar 'round here," Miles muttered, returning to his problem. He began to search every inch of the large stable for signs of bedcovers or cooking utensils. The stacks of hay and bags of oats lined the far inside walls. Then he noticed two loose boards. Quickly, he pulled at them. There was Bounty, staring at him.

"Mister Bounty, I gotta talk ta you," Miles said kindly, stepping into the small, closed-off space, crowded with old bags, blankets, and wood pieces chiseled into odd-looking faces.

"Gotta git me tings together for de woods," Bounty growled as if dismissing the boy.

"I want you ta help me and Mama Cee," Miles said right out. "We want to git 'way from here by tomorrow night."

Bounty's eyes pierced Miles' face.

"Ye got yo' nerve comin' heah," the slave tracker said. "Don't ye reckon I tell Marse Gency? How ye tink I hep?"

"I jest know," Miles answered, not sure. "You helped me one time and I got maps and all for us ta go by."

"What 'bout de dogs?" Bounty quizzed.

Miles dropped his head to the question, knowing that only a good-sense answer would make Bounty listen.

"Scent be cold by de next day if we go at nighttime."

"Ye'll nebber fool good trackin' dogs like dat," Bounty said.

Miles waited.

"Best dogs in dat pen out dere," the old man spoke again, watching the boy.

"But if we git goin' early, mayhap we find somewhar ta hide 'fore dey catch up," Miles contended.

Finally, the old man coughed out, "Be ready ta leave de woods 'morrow night—I come ta ye," Bounty ordered with a wave of his hand.

Miles was still trembling with gladness and fear when he kindled a fire and lit the candle that night.

"Dat's what Elijah meant—ask Bounty," he said.

Suddenly someone knocked on the door. Miles rushed and pulled the door open—to gusty air. Not a soul appeared nearby either. He scrambled between the cabins and looked to the rear. A short, stocky form was fading into the bushes near the beginning of the great house yard. At first he suspected that Macon had been spying for Ol' Miss, but the shadowy form could not have belonged to Macon—too short.

Something was terribly wrong, but he didn't know exactly what. Weary and confused now, he tucked his head down and lifted his foot to clear the doorway. That's when he spied a folded piece of paper, stuck in the corner of the doorjamb. He yanked it loose and rushed to the candle, closing the door at the same time.

"Meet me in the barn," the printed note said. At the bottom was what looked like Elijah's sign, but there was no faint, curly line trailing after the circled star.

"Did dey catch Elijah and now dey tryin' to catch me?" he asked. "Bounty know 'bout dis? Naw, Bounty don't know."

The boy had to think, and think fast.

"Since it don't say when," he figured to himself, "dey be

watchin' dat ol' barn 'til I show up." The field-hand talk seemed to protect him somehow. "Gotta stay 'way from dat barn, but what else can I do?" his mind wondered, working through every possibility.

Mama Cee pushed her way into the cabin and into his deep thoughts.

"Miles," she said, first off. "I never thought Marse Gency was low enough to do this to the old—"

The boy quickly took her work-worn hands and kissed them.

"Mama Cee, we be fine, real fine," he laughed, twirling her around after the dancing fashion at the great house. She laughed, embarrassed at her unsteady steps.

"I be back, I be hungry, you start on de eats," he said, getting out of her sight.

By the time she peeped out of the doorway, he had almost made it to the great house back door.

"Marse Gency," he yelled at the top of his voice. "Marse Gen-cy!"

Macon answered the door, holding a lamp. "Have you gone addled in the head?" the trainer screamed in his most important manner.

"I got ta see Marse Gency," Miles said just as loud.

"What business have you with the master?" Macon asked, annoyed.

"You jest want ta take it 'way from me—tell 'im 'bout me," Miles accused and yelled again, "Marse Gen-cy!"

Gency Tillery appeared behind Macon. Ol' Miss stood behind her husband.

"Take what away from you?" Gency Tillery asked curiously. There was still talk of uprisings in the countryside. No master could afford to ignore the slightest bit of information.

Miles could hardly keep a straight face at the sight of Macon jumping around to avoid standing in front of the master and mistress.

"Take dis, Marse Gency, sir," Miles said and stretched out the folded paper. "I seen a stranger lil' while ago. He left dis paper in my do'."

"What does it say?" the slaveholder asked, speaking directly to Miles and peering at the bold block letters.

"Paper can't talk, Marse Gency, sir," Miles said as if Gency Tillery should have known better. "I don't know what it got on it. You say you give gold to folks who tell you dey see strangers. Ain't never been no paper like dis down dere, 'cept what dat stranger leave. You gonna give me dat piece o' gold, Marse Gency, sir?" Miles asked, hanging on to his act.

"I keep my promises, boy," the slaveholder said, speaking directly to Miles again. "But I have to think on it—you did right to come to me."

With that out of the way, Gency Tillery and Ol' Miss left Macon to dismiss the boy. Neither of them had acted like they remembered him, though he sensed that they knew about the note already.

Miles and Macon locked eyes. Finally, Macon turned away without a word. Miles ran back to the quarters feeling that he had thrown the betrayer off the scent. He did not care if he got the gold piece or not. Masters did not have to keep promises.

# Chapter 13

The next morning, Davidson and McCain stood by while nine old folks were moved to the woods. Kinfolk were allowed to help tote the few odds and ends to the flimsy dwellings.

"You start wailing 'round here, I'll beat tar out of you," Davidson threatened. So none of the beloved old folks made a fuss when they said good-bye to their families and friends.

"Mama Cee!" some of the small children called, not understanding why she was being sent away. The old woman kept a straight back until the mothers took the children inside the cabins.

"Y'all bring the children to see us," she said to various ones.

That the scattered sheds had no chimneys for warmth or for cooking was not surprising to Miles. He knew, now, all there was to know about slavery. From birth to old age, people were treated like they were not people. Bounty sat in his claimed doorway.

"How you do, Mister Bounty?" Miles asked, thinking about their secret.

"Uh-huh," Bounty said, nodding his head.

Mama Cee could not be told. The old and feeble settled into the windowless sheds as best they could.

Mama Cee and those who had more strength went about laying down mattresses and sharing their meager belongings.

Davidson looked on, unconcerned. The field hands would refer to this sad occasion as the "from now on" day for a long time. Davidson's doom and Gency Tillery's doom would pass through their mouths for this cruelty.

On his way to the stable, a certain restlessness and sadness stirred in Miles' chest.

"Wish I could free everybody 'round here," he thought, feeling guilty that he would soon leave the families in slavery, especially the old folks and Dempsey.

That evening, Miles didn't go to the woods until family and friends had seen after the old folks. He met them coming back from the sheds.

"It jest so bad on 'em," one of them remarked.

They had had but a little time to sleep before the "from now on" day. Now this extra burden had already begun to wear them down.

He lit a candle and found Mama Cee's shed in shambles. She hovered in the far corner. A knife had split her mattress in two. Corn shucks lay scattered about. Her head wrap was torn apart.

"They took it, son," she told him quietly. "It was dark in here—I couldn't see them, but they took it."

"The secret," he confirmed.

"Yes."

"Where was it?" he asked.

"Sewed in my head wrap."

He didn't want to know what she had held over Ol' Miss's head for years. He just sat beside her on the dirt floor and held her hand.

"I had papers on Ol' Miss's first marriage," she volunteered. "Gency didn't know she married before him. She never did d'vorce that first husband. Long as I had that she couldn't let anybody sell me and you. I told her somebody know where to find them papers if somethin' happen to me."

"How'd you get the papers?" he asked.

"Found 'em among her things when she say she was gonna sell me before I get too old. Readin' servant tell me what they say. When she find out they were missin', he run off."

Marriage papers and divorces had no meaning for Miles. No one in the great house or the quarters had ever said anything about such papers. He would ask Elijah about these things, one day.

"I never woulda used them papers against her," Mama Cee declared. The boy waited for her to ramble on about the wrongdoings of Ol' Miss. "You know I never hurt nobody," she said in the end.

"Yes, ma'am," Miles said. She must have been easy pickings for whoever tore the place apart. The bottle of ink and the maps were in his pocket—a good thing. Miles didn't know what he would have done if they had hurt her.

He took her hand and told her about Elijah's visit but not about Bounty. Their journey was close at hand. She heaved herself up from the floor like a much younger woman.

"Got to fix my head wrap back on my head," she sang.

Miles stuffed their few articles of clothing in a burlap bag. He crammed the feathered straw hat in the bag. The flour sack he rolled up and stuffed in the bag too.

They sat down among the corn shucks and waited. A growling and rumbling noise stole out of Miles' stomach.

"You hungry?" she asked.

Before he could answer, she said, "I'm hungry too."

"Hush, Mama Cee." He touched her arm. They trained their ears at the door. Three taps echoed throughout the almost empty dwelling. Miles held his breath, tiptoed across, and opened the door.

"Time," Bounty rasped a whisper. "Put out dat candle. Git yo' Mama Cee and tings. Y'all gwine on dat wagon," Bounty said quickly, pointing in the moonlight. The boy did not see the wagon, but he believed Bounty.

"Mama Cee," he whispered through the moonlit door. She ironed her hands over her mouth. "Everything all right," he assured her.

"Just wish I could say somethin' to the folks I been knowin' so long," she said.

He grabbed her hand and the bag at the same time.

Save for the wind blowing the bushes and trees, not a sound was heard as Miles and Bounty helped Mama Cee onto the wagon bed of corn shuck mattresses. A burlap bag of fodder and a jug of water lay at her feet along with their blankets.

Bounty sat beside Miles on the wagon seat and pulled on the reins.

"Dat's Big Red!" Miles blew out between his teeth.

A violent shake of Bounty's head let Miles know that he should shut his mouth.

Just like in his daydreams, Big Red was his for right now. They followed a crooked wagon path unknown to Miles through the woods for about two hours. He did know that they were not traveling in the direction of Wettown or the town of Tillery. The horse seemed to have excellent moonlight vision.

Mama Cee dozed under the blankets.

One tug on the lines and Big Red stopped.

Bounty placed the reins in Miles' hand and eased, noiselessly, onto the ground.

Miles strained his eyes to keep track of the old man, who moved like he was stepping in cotton, some yards away. Then Bounty disappeared to the left, behind a large tree.

"I ain't scared," Miles breathed his old saving words.

He waited two or three minutes, glancing all around. The moon hung suspended in the cloudless sky to their backs now.

"Take dis." Bounty's deep voice broke the silence, scaring Miles witless.

"Take what?" The boy whirled to his right to answer. Not only had Bounty sneaked up on Miles, but the old man had returned from the opposite side of the wagon.

"Ain't go ta scare ye," Bounty said, handing up a wrapped package. "Jest want I should learn ye how to git 'round dese woods d'out folks seeing ye an' heering ye."

Miles took the package. Right away the scent of food filled the air.

"Where you git dis?" Miles asked.

"I be a friend of a friend who know a friend," Bounty said. "Tell ye at safe time. Wake up yo' Mama Cee."

"Eatin' time." Miles patted her shoulder.

He opened the cover of a small pot of smoked meat and rutabagas and three metal spoons. A cloth napkin enfolded three warm, baked white potatoes and a hunk of cheese.

"Smells good," Mama Cee said when Miles passed the pot to her.

"Got bowls, under me mattress," Bounty told her.

She dipped a bowl of the rutabagas and meat for Bounty, then for herself. The rest was left in the pot for Miles. He promptly ate out of the pot, more with his hand than the spoon. It seemed that he was always hungry or afraid that he was going to be hungry. At last they drank from the jug of cool water. The boy leaned back, full to the brim. Mama Cee dozed off again. Miles was too excited to feel sleepy. Nero's shirt scratched his itchy back.

They rode on for two more hours before Bounty tugged at the lines.

"See if ye can take dat bridle off Big Red, Miles," Bounty suggested.

Miles hit the ground running to remove the harness from his favorite horse. Big Red was a favorite of Ol' Miss. Gency Tillery liked to ride Big Red too. He had been so busy thinking about freedom, the wants and wishes of Gency Tillery and his wife never crossed his mind. Surely they would be angry about losing Big Red and him.

"Mister Bounty," Miles asked, "you think dey gonna set the dogs on us?"

"Dey will," Bounty said.

Mama Cee stirred. "Dogs? Y'all hear dogs?" she panicked.

"Hesh dat fuss," Bounty ordered kindly. "No dogs. I fix dey noses. Dey can't scent us in a great while—three, four days."

"We be gone by den," Miles told Mama Cee, but thinking about learning how to fix a dog's nose.

"Marse Gency tell me ta give ye dis gold piece," Bounty said, smiling and offering the shiny coin.

Miles grabbed the coin. Elijah had told him about money, but he had never seen one piece of it. He looked at the coin from every angle in the moonlight.

"He say for me ta take ye ta spend it t'morrow in Tillery," Bounty joked. "Ye want ta go back?"

Miles laughed and heard the coin clink against the ink

bottle in his pocket. He pulled one of the mattresses from the wagon. He and Bounty took turns sleeping until the morning sun peeped through the woods. The March wind had died down some. It was going to be a warm day.

The boy opened the bag of fodder for Big Red. The horse ate some and began to nibble at the tender spring grass.

"We be out dese woods nigh," Bounty said.

"I know. Den us be on a train," Miles said. "We gonna be slaves you takin' somewhar," he added, remembering the map and his trip to the breaking ground.

"I 'clare, boy," Bounty said, full of life. "I knowed ye got sense."

"You gonna hafta sell Big Red."

Bounty did not say anymore.

"You ever seen a bill of sale?" Miles asked, not mentioning Elijah's instructions.

"Shore," Bounty answered. "I sell tings for Marse Gency an' dem."

"Well, we sell Big Red in Dillon—den us git on de train," Miles said, pulling the paper from between his shirts.

"Set down, 'Bill of Sale' for de horse," Bounty directed Miles to write. "I be selling for Mist' Barnhill. He in Virginny, long time from heah." Bounty traced his finger across the top of the paper.

Miles aimed the feather, using the wagon seat's flat surface. *Bill of Sale* flowed from the pen.

Not showing surprise that Miles could write, Bounty

went on with, "Set down 'one horse, three-year-old—stallion—twenty-five dollars.'"

Miles suspected that maybe Bounty could read and write some and that the old man had seen hundreds of bills of sale for slaves during his tracking days. Ten minutes passed before the letters were joined together to Miles' satisfaction. He surveyed the ink-wet document, reading it aloud several times.

Each time Bounty nodded his head vigorously and said, "Dat's plenty good—plenty good."

Mama Cee just smiled. She seemed quiet. Her legs stretched out in the wagon bed. They drank the remaining water. The horse drank from a nearby stream.

By midmorning, Big Red pulled them out of the woods and into an open field. Tops of buildings poked up on the other side. That meant they had to travel downhill.

Miles looked at the sky. The sun was on his right. They were heading north.

"Kenyon," he said to no one. "We goin' ta Dillon on Elijah's map."

"Us find eats dere," Bounty said.

They ended up at the livery stables.

"Bounty!" a big, robust white man called from inside. "See you bagged two of 'em. What was that old one running away from?" he asked, studying Mama Cee's downcast face.

"Gwine back ta Virginny, Mist' John," Bounty said, making no account of the man's question with a friendly grin.

Miles acted as much like a slave as he could. He would have felt better had Bounty put shackles on him. Mama Cee was too old to jump out of the wagon and run.

People passed, giving him and Mama Cee a curious eye. Many seemed sympathetic. They seemed to know about Bounty being a slave tracker.

"Yassar, gotta sell dis horse an' git dat train nigh," Bounty told the man.

"Price?" the man asked, eyeing Big Red, ignoring Miles and Mama Cee.

"Twenty-five," Bounty said, showing the bill of sale.

Miles' heart leaped. "Suppose it don't look right," he thought, wanting to read the man's face but wary of looking at him.

"Mister Barnhill, huh?" the man accepted, like he knew Barnhill.

"He up dere tradin' and sellin'," Bounty added.

When this tidbit of information put a look of comfort on the man's face, Miles could see that the black man and the white man were striving to outsmart each other.

"Dis horse run fast—good temper too," Bounty justified the price.

"Mister Barnhill set a high price, Bounty," John said, pleading poormouth.

"Well, he say 'give em de wagon,'" Bounty bargained.

"Sold!" the man said, smiling like he had won a game. Miles took no notice of Big Red. The man called John patted the horse's face. "He is gentle," he said.

Bounty threw the reins under the wagon seat. The man took hold of the bridle and guided Big Red into the dingy stables, leaving them with their burlap bag of things.

Bounty stuffed twenty-five dollars in his pocket.

"Walk 'side me," the old man told them on their way down the dirt street. They smelled sausage cooking.

"Hungry," Mama Cee said.

"Me too," Miles echoed.

"Wait," Bounty answered them.

They had to wait almost twenty minutes while the line to the link sausage cooker's pit grew longer and longer. Cooks, maids, and housekeepers of every color clamored to get the attention of the barrel-bellied man in the greasy white apron.

"Smell so good," Mama Cee murmured.

Folks who were buying raw sausage were given their parcel of sausage tied in brown paper right away.

Nearby, Miles spotted what looked to be the last of somebody's root cellar. Turnips, rutabagas, and white potatoes were mixed in one barrel.

Finally, the sausage cooker gave Bounty his warm bundle of link sausage, wrapped in brown paper too—grease already staining the package.

Just then, the rumble of a train jarred the ground. The old man tossed the food to Miles and rushed to pick among the root barrel.

Soon Miles and Mama Cee followed Bounty to the train station, located further down the dirt street.

"What you say, Bounty?" a man with a peculiar-looking hat joked, at the head of the train.

"Can't say nothin'," Bounty joked back, shelling off some of the money.

"You know where to go," the man said to Bounty, counting the money and flicking a glare at Miles and Mama Cee at the same time.

Another man in the same blue hat strolled up as Miles and Mama Cee followed Bounty toward the end of the train.

Miles wondered if Bounty heard one of them say, "Best runaway tracker in the south."

One small window in the musty compartment gave them the opportunity to see the outside. Miles couldn't bring himself to look. They were by themselves. He was gladder now than ever that he had asked Bounty to help him. Still, there was something mysterious about the slave tracker.

The train jiggled along, puffing smoke.

Exhausted, the three of them searched here and there in the dim light. A nailed-to-the-floor bench with a wooden back was long enough to seat two of them. Miles sat on the bag of things.

"Somebody just been here," Mama Cee commented, with a crinkle in her nose.

"Uh-huh, dey got off," Bounty agreed, flipping his thumb in the opposite direction of where they were riding.

Not only did Miles detect the scent of unwashed bodies, but the presence of sadness, left behind, was almost unbearable.

"Slaves," he thought to himself. Two ragged blankets lay in the corner.

Mama Cee doled out the sausage and raw root vegetables.

"Keep up strength," was all she had to say to make Miles eat the unpeeled rutabagas. He bit into the bittersweet vegetable and took a bite of sausage. Slowly, the smell of sausage disguised the other odors in the compartment.

Mama Cee and Bounty finished quickly. They leaned back and closed their eyes.

The boy had questions, as always. He wanted to know what Bounty had done to keep the dogs from being able to scent a trail. The slave tracker seemed to know as much as Elijah but in a different way. He spread out the maps.

"Mister Bounty." He risked giving the old man some sketchy information about the maps. "We git ta Virginny den us cut cross to de west and round some hills."

"I know whar us gwine," Bounty snapped. "I leave ye at dem hills."

"Leave us?" Mama Cee asked curiously.

Silence.

Miles was disturbed that Bounty was going to leave them; he didn't know exactly where. Did Bounty want them to get caught? Did Bounty know about Elijah?

"How you know where us be goin'? Why ain't you tell me?" he asked forcefully.

"Ye ain't asked," Bounty said, quietly disarming the boy.

Miles groaned inwardly at his foolishness. He wondered if Bounty would have volunteered information if he had asked. Suspicion beat in the boy's chest.

"Mister Bounty," he began again, this time without irritation. "How you know where us be goin'?"

The old man sat up and twisted around to look at the boy.

"Done sum trackin' in me day, boy. Most runners don't go de way us be goin'—ain't know how. Lemme tell ye, dese hills so high ye got ta walk 'round." Bounty stretched his arms high and reached around a wide circle. "Dere's one, two, three of 'em."

Miles stopped thinking that Bounty was trying to hide something. The boy stirred his memory for the drawing of three hills. Elijah had told him that he would meet them after the third hill. The third hill was shaped like a man's face. Elijah said it would take two or three days to get there from Dillon. They had to pass through a place called Sharpes, North Carolina.

Miles lay back on the bag of things. He could do more than just dream about freedom now. There was the freedom path that Elijah had mapped out. He inhaled deeply.

# Chapter 14

Mostly, Mama Cee's face had been like a blank piece of paper since the beginning of their journey. She seemed so much older too, eyeing his every move. Often, she looked like she had been crying, but he had not seen her cry.

The sound of the rickety-rackety train wheels wore on and on before Miles spoke again. He could not stand the two voiceless folks any longer.

"You gonna be free too, Mister Bounty," the boy directed his peppy voice.

Silence.

Miles did not know what made him say such a thing. After all, Bounty's job had been to keep slaves away from freedom. The boy's teeth clamped down at the thought of Bounty putting shackles on him.

"What ails you, son?" Mama Cee asked in a shaky voice.

Miles stopped grinding his teeth.

"Ain't nothin'," he answered.

"Yes 'tis," Bounty said.

"You ain't nothin' but a stinkin' tracker," Miles accused the old man.

Mama Cee hollered, "Where is your manners? Mister Bounty's a grown man—old, too. I reckon you think you grown."

Miles looked away in silence.

"Miss Cee, lemme collect my say-so's ta ye." Bounty slipped his words out, asking her to listen to his story.

Miles felt a bit of shame when Mama Cee turned her complete attention to Bounty, leaving him to learn a lesson in good manners.

The old man went on with, "Time, time, and time agin, I go back and steal de folks I track. Den I lead dem to freedom wid money I gits for trackin' dem de furst time. White folks ain't catch me yit."

Miles cut in instantly, "You ain't lead me ta freedom. You take me to de breakin' ground and I—"

Mama Cee spoke up, ignoring Miles.

"Mister Bounty," she said, trusting the old man, "I can't excuse my boy's bad manners, but I never did hear nothin' good 'bout you on Gency Tillery's place."

Miles watched Bounty squeeze out a chesty laugh. It seemed that the old man's beard had grown whiter and stragglier.

"Yassar," Bounty said at the end of his laugh. "All big masters say me de best. Gency Tillery toss me 'way ta de woods, too." A sly grin left a twinkle in Bounty's wide-set eyes.

"He glad 'bout what he done," Miles thought. Mama Cee used to hate him too. Now she eyed him as if he was a brand-new man. At last, the fog that draped around the mysterious Bounty had lifted.

The rickety-rackety noise from the train wheels slowed

down and the wheels ceased to turn.

Bounty pointed to the window.

Miles walked to the grimy pane and peeped out—to see only sky.

"Dis train gonna fall off," the boy warned, tiptoeing back to the bench, thinking his weight would topple the train off the tracks.

"Bridge," Bounty said, not worried.

Mama Cee smiled.

This one word put Miles at ease. He looked out of the window again, this time straining to see the bridge that was holding the train up. He could not.

The train was suspended between earth and sky for what seemed to be hours. They could hear men shouting to each other further up the line of coaches.

That day, the train came to a standstill three more times. Two of the times they were able to get off and stretch. Bounty found drinking water and poor food like dried beef and stale bread.

By three o'clock on the third day, the train pulled into Sharpes's depot.

No one paid attention as they stepped down from the dingy slave coach. Having spent so many hours in the shade, they squinted in the bright sunshine.

The three of them followed the tracks toward the main part of the bustling depot.

"I find eats 'n water, folks know me," Bounty said, leaving Miles and Mama Cee standing in front of a ramshackle building. They inched out of the sun under a small awning that covered the front of the building.

From there, Miles and Mama Cee gawked at the passers-by that seemed to be in a great hurry to enter a sturdier-looking building across the narrow lane.

Slowly, Miles ceased gazing at the men, women, and children and noticed yellow and black placards someone had pasted onto the walls of the building where he and Mama Cee were standing.

The bold letters on the placards caught his eye. He pretended that something was wrong with his eyes as he rubbed them and glanced at the words. "WANTED" one card said with tiny lettering below. Miles stole looks long enough to read:

REWARD

ONE HUNDRED DOLLARS for slave named ELIJAH.
About 35 years of age, INTELLIGENT.
May be able to read.
A master at ELUDING. Last seen in Virginia.
John Cobb, Wettown, South Carolina.

Miles didn't know what to think now. Beads of sweat ran down his back.

"What it say, son?" Mama Cee asked before he could get his thoughts straight about Elijah. She had stolen looks at his stolen looks.

"It say somebody runnin'," he answered hastily, sifting through scores of moving bodies for Bounty.

"Come here, boy," a nasal voice interrupted. Miles and Mama Cee flinched just a little when they pivoted to see two stringy-legged white men a few yards away.

Miles looked away like he had not heard. Mama Cee did the same.

"Bounty, Bounty," Miles said to himself.

"You heered me, boy," the man ordered. Both of them walked under the awning.

"Waitin' for my master," Miles excused himself for not obeying.

"He be right back," Mama Cee chimed.

"Don't see no master, boy," the second said, ignoring Mama Cee. "You come with me quiet like, boy."

Miles did not pull away when the man grabbed his arms and tied his hands in front of him with a heavy rope. He smiled at Mama Cee and shook his head. She understood that the men might hurt her if she protested.

Before he knew it, the back of his shirt was snatched up, his body propelled toward the building he had seen so many folks entering. Surprisingly, the doorway cleared to a breezeway. An open court lay on the other side. People milled around a raised platform.

"We oughta take his shirt off and smear a little lard on his back," Miles heard from one of the men who held his arm. He couldn't see their faces.

"Make him look healthy and bring more money," the other agreed.

"Dey stealin' me," Miles realized. "And dat de auction block, like Bounty said."

A young woman with a baby clutched to her bosom faced the buyers and spectators.

"Two for the price of one," a beefy man with a bow tie was saying. Shirtless slave men and boys sat on the ground. Several slaveholders stood watch, waiting to sell their unhappy victims.

A big hand jerked at his shirttail.

"Dere's my master," Miles suddenly yelled at the top of his lungs, looking over the crowd to the opposite end of the court. "Master Dempsey, Master Dempsey!"

Miles took off on a run toward an imaginary master, shedding the loose rope. Glancing over his shoulder, he saw that he was not being followed. The crowd turned back to the auctioneer.

Miles disappeared through another door resembling the kidnappers' door. He was right—another breezeway. He raced to the end, accidentally falling into Bounty's arms, almost knocking the old man off of his feet.

"Cee tell me 'bout ye," Bounty said, straightening up, catching his breath.

"Yassar," Miles puffed out, keeping in step with Bounty through the empty doorway. "Mister Bounty, dey got a reward out 'bout Elijah," he puffed in a whisper, out of Mama Cee's earshot.

"Know 'bout dat," Bounty laughed now. "Elijah smart-o."

Mama Cee was standing in the street, holding an extra sack. She cried weakly at the sight of him. No one would ever steal her because of her age. Still, to him, she was the most beautiful person he had ever seen. He had to hold on to his wits. Soon, Bounty would leave them.

"We got to go with you next time, Mister Bounty," Mama Cee pleaded.

Miles was glad to see the old man nod to agree with her. She looked like she felt better.

The sun was setting when Bounty slipped some folded money to another blue-hatted man. They found seats in a slave coach the same as before. The train picked up speed. They were heading farther west.

Bounty put a sly grin on his face and sectioned off a piece of roasted lamb with his knife. A jug of water sat under the bench.

"Taste so good," Mama Cee complimented. "How you get it, Mister Bounty?"

"Not steal—pay money," Bounty snickered. But then he reached in the sack and yanked out one half of a pound cake made like the ones at the great house.

"Steal dis," he said. "Cook steal me money—I steal dis."

Miles held his breath, expecting Mama Cee to tell the old man that stealing was wrong. She didn't.

"Yassar, I know she steal. She know me steal," the old man said, ending his fun. He divided the cake into thick slices with his knife.

Within two days the cake was gone. When they boarded the last train, there was no money left except for Miles' gold coin. Tillery, Dillon, Sharpes, and Jonesbridge were behind them now. They were tired and sore to the bone from being jerked about from one side of the track to the other. Mama Cee looked tired. She broke out in fits of sneezing from time to time, even after Miles piled his blanket on her too.

"Be dere nigh," Bounty said to no one in particular as the last train slowed down. He did not say anything about leaving them.

"Den de hills," Miles thought.

The sinking sunlight showed lines and arrows on the map that Miles studied again. Humps stood for the three hills Bounty had mentioned. The last hump had a bold X marked where Elijah would appear.

"Mountains," Miles thought, remembering the word from his friend's reading lessons at the breaking ground. "I reckon I ought to tear dis up now," the boy said.

"Safe. Keep," Bounty said with a wave of his hand.

Late that night, a chill fell over the coach. Mama Cee started coughing.

Miles left his bag of things and wrapped both of their ratty blankets around her shoulders and feet. Since Bounty had vacated the bench and sprawled on the floor, she seemed more comfortable.

"Thank you, son," she said and dozed off.

Warm sunshine came through the window the next morning. Mama Cee rose from the bench.

"Got to stretch my legs," she said tiredly.

Bounty paced the length and width of the coach several times, keeping his balance on the unsteady flooring.

"Dis make ye strong," he said, eyeing Miles.

Every muscle in Miles' body ached, but he jumped up to pace anyway.

"We be dere soon, huh, Bounty?" Miles asked, concerned for Mama Cee.

"Yassar," Bounty said.

"What time of day is it?" Miles asked, remembering the old man's watch.

"Can't tell," Bounty said shortly.

"Show me," Miles said, knowing that Bounty could tell time.

"Watch gone," Bounty said sheepishly. "Git rid of it back dere so dey'll let us off de train away from folks."

Mama Cee cleared her throat. Miles fell silent. Bounty had sold his precious watch for them and this good deed was not to be discussed, ever. Bounty was risking his life for them, Miles now understood.

Miles dug in his pocket for the gold piece.

"Take dis," he offered. Bounty snatched the coin like he had forgotten that it existed. The boy had no idea how much the coin was worth.

The train wobbled into midmorning like a loud mule-drawn cart. Inside, there was a calmness that each of them could claim as his own.

For Miles, every turn of the wheels brought him closer to freedom. The closer he drew, the more hideous the word *slave* became. At the same time, thoughts of reading books and newspapers and telling his own feet where to go helped him override the word *slave*.

Mama Cee's coughing shattered his thoughts.

"I'm all right, son," she wheezed out when he patted her back. There was no more food or water to give her. It was about noon by the look of the sun.

"Be dere nigh," Bounty said to comfort the boy. "Dis train run, run, run," Bounty said.

Finally, the wheels screeched to a standstill in the middle of a wood. Miles slid the door open. Everywhere trees sprouted buds and baby leaves. Dogwood blossoms waved in a light breeze.

This time there were no steps so Mama Cee sat in the doorway with her legs swinging over the rocky ground. Quickly Bounty and Miles lifted her to a standing position. The train picked up speed again.

"Dis way," Bounty said, rushing them into the woods. Miles slipped his hand under Mama Cee's arm. Grayish mountains loomed in every direction. Yet he knew from the map that these were not the mountains Elijah wrote about.

"We free yet?" Mama Cee asked.

"No, ma'am," Miles answered, wishing he had good news.

Bounty would be leaving them soon. That fact took all of his attention now.

"Hunkle down," Bounty said, pointing to a tree.

"Me and Mama Cee got to go 'fore dark," Miles said, watching Bounty pace to and fro. The boy's mind hastened to figure out how they were going to eat and sleep. Their mountains were some miles away. He didn't know how many.

Mama Cee spread her blankets on the damp ground. A deep cough bent her body double. She sat down heavily.

"Ye wait," Bounty said after a while, moving off.

"Where you goin', Mister Bounty?" Miles screamed a whisper at the old man's back.

"Ye safe—ye wait," Bounty said over his shoulder and kept going.

"He'll be back," Mama Cee said, not showing fear.

"We can't stay here 'til it get dark. He so shut-mouth," Miles complained to her.

"A shut mouth can say a heap," she said.

The boy let that wise saying settle for a while. Bounty was quiet. Before, if someone had told him the old man assisted slaves to freedom, Miles never would have believed it.

# Chapter 15

Miles sat beside Mama Cee and rubbed the back of her hand. Neither he nor Bounty had mentioned her cough. The boy noticed, though, the old man wincing when a deep cough bent her over.

Miles found himself circling the trees. Something kept picking at him to think that Bounty was not coming back. Maybe something had happened to him.

"Don't you worry, Mama Cee," he said to her. "We gonna be dere soon."

The light wind had turned chilly when the sound of what seemed to be a wounded animal blasted through the woods, scaring Mama Cee off the blanket.

The boy pulled off a low-hanging limb to defend them as best he could.

Noisily, a mule-like animal emerged with Bounty sauntering alongside, tugging on the reins. Dragging on the ground was a litter, attached to the beast's harness.

"Burro, me buy," the old man smiled out, identifying the animal. "We go now."

"Thank you, Mister Bounty," was all Miles could say. Hundreds of questions strained to pop out of his mouth. Bounty would do his best to evade a direct answer, so he didn't ask.

With Mama Cee on the litter and the blankets tucked around her, they set out through the woods, away from the train tracks. Foot trails rose before them for a little while. Below them the tops of trees shimmered in the late afternoon sunlight. Then the wild countryside snared their shoes and entangled them in vine creepers. He and Bounty worked to steer the stubborn burro through the less dense brambles and bushes.

Miles took another look at his map. Hunger and thirst began to creep up on him. He knew that if the old man could have found something to eat or drink he would have done so.

After about a mile, the scent of burning wood filled the air. Bounty braced himself against the reins with all his might in order to stop the burro. Somewhere in the distance dogs barked.

Bounty sniffed the air and cupped his ear upwind.

Miles held his breath. "Trackin' dogs," was his only thought.

"Dem ain't trackin' dogs," Bounty disagreed, reading the boy's thoughts. "Trackin' dogs howl some."

A mile or so later the setting sun blazed in the western sky. Miles watched the burro pause to chomp on the newly budded plants. They were going downhill now.

Wood smoke curled up to their noses again.

"Water," Mama Cee said.

Miles dreaded to hear her weak voice. He looked at Bounty. Bounty looked at the burro.

"Burro find water," he said. "Wait."

"She ain't gonna wait," Miles uttered firmly. "Ought ta be water where dat smoke is," he added, walking away.

"Miles," Mama Cee called on his third or fourth step.

Bounty grunted when the boy ran back to her.

"Wait," she said, softly. "Bounty know 'bout these things."

Bounty explained, "When de burro git a full belly, he find water all right. He smell water. I tell ye dese tings 'cause ye needs ta know."

"Yassar, Mister Bounty," Miles said respectfully.

The old man nodded his head like he understood Miles was worried sick about Mama Cee.

In the meantime, Miles decided to snap off the tenderest plants by hand. He piled this foodstuff in front of the animal.

"Dat's good," Bounty exclaimed, tying the reins to a strong sapling and snapping the tender plants too.

Fairly soon the burro's stomach pouched out on both sides.

Bounty untied the slack reins. Amazingly, the burro pulled off like someone had given it a map to the next watering hole. Miles and Bounty followed on either side, each holding a rein.

Mama Cee seemed comfortable as the litter zigzagged through the overgrown bushes. The burro stopped and raised its head.

Water was plinking down from somewhere. The three of them heard it.

Quickly, the burro pulled beyond a mess of tangled bushes and scrubby trees on Miles' side to a small pool of water. A steady drip from above replaced the water that spilled over the ledge.

Miles filled the empty jug and handed it to Mama Cee, relieved that she was strong enough to sit up and drink. He and Bounty caught handfuls of the dripping water, and he attempted to fill the hungry space in his stomach with deep swallows.

The sun was all the way down now. A dim light peeped up from below.

"I'm goin' down dere ta see if I can find eats," Miles said, stepping off.

"Mayhap slavers down dere," Bounty warned. "Dey ain't know me in dese parts."

"I'm goin' anyhow," Miles said, determined.

The old man watched the boy turn sideways and half slide, half walk down the steep hill. This was the dream Miles had dreamed many times. The dream that showed him taking care of Mama Cee.

Bounty waited and watched Mama Cee.

"Us git on good," he said to comfort her.

Creeping and crawling things screeched and buzzed. It was springtime in the mountains too, except the air seemed dryer.

Faintly came the sound of Miles heaving his way up the hill.

"Found dese," he said, out of breath, when he saw the old man.

Bounty reached to grab a hand.

"Naw," Miles said, taking turns to push something in front of him with one hand and holding on to the vine creepers with the other. Finally, the boy pulled himself to level ground.

"Got eggs," he beamed at them. "A pot too—dog's pot."

He could feel the two old folks' smiles.

"Us oughta go on 'til ain't no lights down there. Den us cook," the boy suggested.

"Ye right, boy," Bounty agreed.

About a mile farther, Miles gathered a few small rocks to hold the pot of water over the fire Bounty kindled.

In no time, they were peeling ten boiled eggs. Miles popped down three and drank some of the water from the jug. Mama Cee and Bounty finished the rest.

"I sleep here," Bounty said, nestling on the side of a boulder.

That left Miles to stomp out the fire, unharness the burro, and tie the reins to a sturdy tree. He dragged Mama Cee's litter to a boulder of her own. Soon she slept peacefully.

Bounty was snoring when he went to sleep. The next morning at sunup, Miles awoke to find that the old man was still snoring. Mama Cee had thrown one of the blankets on him.

The weather got warmer over the next few days, but Mama Cee's cough got worse. They had been traveling for four days when she began to feel warm to the touch at times.

She made no account of her illness by insisting that she walk some.

"Get my strength back," she convinced them.

The map showed they were almost to the mountain that resembled a man's head.

Miles and Bounty took turns scrounging for food and water. For the most part they had been able to find eggs and spring onions and a few potatoes from root cellars. Not once did they arouse dogs or the white people who lived near the base of the mountains.

"They got slaves 'round here?" the boy wanted to know from Bounty when they rested at the base of the second mountain.

"Slave farms," Bounty answered like he did not want to talk further.

"Slave farms?"

Bounty cut his eye at Mama Cee, hoping she would stop the boy's questions. Her look in another direction told him she was not going to do that.

"What is a slave fa—"

"Ye know whar Marse Gency buy Big Red?" Bounty rushed on. "De horse farm be whar dey breed nothin' but horses. Slave farm do de same—nothin' but slaves."

"Dey raise 'em ta work and ta sell," the boy thought to himself, "like horses and mules."

On the fifth day, before sunup, Bounty told him, "Ye git water, boy."

"Yassar," Miles answered gladly. He and Bounty had been able to take an old hen from a coop the evening before.

Mama Cee had been well enough to pluck it. While doing so, she brought back her childhood days that she had never discussed with Miles. He knew very little about her life before he was sold to Gency Tillery.

"I was just a little ol' thing when my mama showed me how pluck a chicken," she smiled. "We saved feathers—for pillows."

"Mama Cee," he dared to ask. "Where were you born?"

"On the old Jemison place. You passed by there when they took you to the breakin' ground. Ol' Miss was his wife's niece, but her folks didn't have nothin' but hard times."

"I'll finish," the boy said, pulling feathers by the last bit of sunlight. He had learned how to draw the intestines too.

Bounty cut the chicken in half and boiled it with wild onions. For fear the chicken would spoil, they ate it all.

"Best chicken I ever ate," Mama Cee praised Bounty. "And Miles, you the best chicken plucker. Just remember that and what a fine young man you turned out to be when you get to freedom."

"When *we* get to freedom," Miles corrected her, feeling

proud to be called a young man. "All I want to do is find Elijah for us now."

"If you got anything in view to do—do it, do it, do it," she said firmly. She said it in a way that told him he could.

And that became Miles' song.

He made up his own tune and he sang it. He whispered the tune to himself and to the wind. It was a good song and it was his. Mama Cee had given it to him.

Before they bedded down for the night he sang his song to her. They listened to her singing the last of the words.

Late that night, he and Bounty took turns patting her back during her fits of coughing. Her hand felt hot to the touch then. By morning she had cooled off. He watched her sleep quietly with the blankets up to her neck.

"Heah de jug, boy," Bounty said, shoving it into his hands. "I water burro when ye git back."

The watering hole was not far behind them. He took off in a trot, watching and listening to the surrounding area.

Suddenly, he pulled to a stop a few yards from the fresh water. A mountain lion was drinking. He stood still, scared to breathe while the beast drank and then licked itself for what seemed to be hours; then it loped away from him.

He ran and sank his jug into the water as far as possible from the spot the mountain lion drank from. He watched the gurgling water fill his jug.

On his way back the boy could see Bounty fiddling with the burro's harness, not paying attention to Mama Cee.

Quickly, he sat the jug down and rushed to turn her face away from the sun.

"Turn me to the light, son," she whispered. He turned her to the sun again.

"To the light, son," she whispered, looking over her shoulder, away from the sun.

Confused, Miles turned her again. She looked for a long time at a light he could not see. Then her eyes closed.

"Naw, Mama Cee," he wailed. "We goin' to freedom— wake up."

Bounty's strong arms pulled him away.

"She gone, Miles," he said.

The boy collapsed, sobbing.

The old man shook him like a rag doll.

"Hesh yo' fuss, slavers come 'fore ye git ta freedom."

"Don't want freedom without Mama Cee, Mister Bounty," Miles said, still crying but silently.

"She say freedom for ye," Bounty said. "Elijah be dere— ain't far."

"Got to bury her somehow, Bounty," Miles said.

"Be honor for me ta do dat," Bounty cut in.

"Dis the day I see Elijah, 'fore dark," the boy said, still thinking about delaying his journey for Mama Cee's burial.

Bounty put the jug of water in the flour sack and slung it over Miles' shoulder. The boy's song clicked in his head. Haltingly, at first, the words trickled out. "If you got anything in view to do—do it, do it, do it."

The next time Bounty's thick voice joined him.

The boy studied his map with words to the song flowing and Bounty's quiet singing, "do it, do it, do it."

The old man hugged him and pointed for him to be on his way.

The boy looked back when he approached a hollow in the lay of the land. He knew that when he entered the hollow, Bounty's voice would be lost to him.

He sang his song one last time and Bounty answered.

Two hours into the hollow Miles drank from the jug. Now he understood why Elijah had advised him to eat and rest all he could. He felt hungry, but strong too.

His eyes became teary every time he thought of Mama Cee. Only her gift of song lessened his grief somewhat. He sang the song again and again.

There were no houses or people about. Deerflies kept him company, buzzing a circle around his head. By late afternoon, a head-shaped mountain bulged from the ground as soon as he climbed out of the hollow.

He scaled the next hill and stood clear of the scattered scrub trees, viewing the valley below. He was supposed to stand under the man's nose, facing northwest—where the big $X$ was on the paper. The sun helped to guide him in that direction where sweeping wind made the trees sing. He saw no one. For a long time the boy paced and traced his steps with the jug of water on his back. Then he climbed higher to get a better view of the valley.

"Miles!" Elijah's familiar voice resounded from freedom side.

"Elijah!" The boy screamed away fear and anger and sadness. He ran-leaped down the hill, arms outstretched, leaving the slave jug and the slave sack behind.

He was going to freedom.